SEVEN

A Novel of Domestic Terrorism

By Jerry Johnson

This book is dedicated to my wife, Julie. She will always be my inspiration.

"Wherever you have weakened states and turmoil, you will have a fertile petri dish for terrorism"

- Robert D. Kaplan
-

It's scary how much of this story could actually come true...

Prologue

Robert Smithson
Journal Entry
Saturday, July 1, 2006

Making Ricin is actually pretty easy. Staying alive while you isolate the peptide, package it, and deliver the poison to your intended victims is the hard part.

Luckily, as a PhD candidate in biochemistry here at the University of North Carolina, I have the necessary skills and the available lab to handle those issues.

Ricin is only one of several "plagues" that I'm about to bring down on Bush, Cheney, and the rest of the stooges in our government that got us involved in the war in Iraq, and that now refuse to bring our troops back home. Better chemistry for better living! Either the government will start withdrawing troops, or the people in charge will suffer the consequences.

Since they brought my Dad back from Iraq in a coffin with a flag draped over it, I've been hearing the voice of God, telling me that I need to do something to get us out of that ridiculous war.

A stupid Green Zone car bombing (so much for that allegedly "safe" area of Iraq) blew my dad into several pieces. Two dead, four injured - just another statistic in the war to preserve our oil interests and generate big bucks for the military industrial complex.

Now I am the FBI's worst nightmare - a domestic terrorist with the training to inflict real harm, and the skills needed to stay out of the clutches of the law enforcement people for some length of time. From my mom, I got my love of science. My dad was a spook. He was a colonel in the army, worked in Delta Force, and then he was seconded to the Defense Intelligence Agency. He taught me about creating false IDs, how to pick locks, create disguises, and the use of explosives and firearms. At 23, I am as well trained as any potential terrorist could be.

I'm taking my inspiration for this campaign from the Bible. Moses was the first terrorist. He, too, heard the voice of God, telling him to go back to Egypt and free his people. The 10 plagues he inflicted on the Egyptians finally forced the Pharaoh to let the Hebrews leave captivity, so Moses led a very successful terrorist campaign.

I'm crazy enough to believe that I'm hearing God, but yet sane enough to know that the voice is probably just my inner justification for the terror I'm about to inflict. No matter. I'm going to follow in Moses' footsteps, and my war of terror is about to begin. "Let my people go" has become my new mantra.

I've been preparing for this for almost six months. I've spent a lot of time creating my weapons, and flying and driving around the country, scouting potential attack locations. I don't know if I'll be as successful as Moses was - but either way, the people of America will know I tried! I do have some scruples - I'm not about to release something like Ebola on the United States. My attacks will be specifically targeted, limited as much as possible to the people involved in getting us into this war. There will be some collateral damage, with some innocent people getting hurt or killed, but hopefully I can hold that problem to a minimum.

I'm sure this journal will eventually be found. The FBI is very thorough, and I'm sure at some point I'll be identified. I hope to never be captured, but I wanted a record of my motives to be out there for everyone to see.

You can call this the New Robert's Rules of Order...

Chapter 1

Robert Smithson
Reagan National Airport, Washington, D.C.
Tuesday, July 4, 2006 2:15 AM

I'm so scared I can't breathe. And every time I force myself to take a breath, the smell of the kerosene and gasoline that I had loaded into the sprayer reminds me that even if I survive this first attempt to attack the United States government, the path I am putting myself on by starting the sprayer will lead to even greater dangers in the future.

Tonight is the kickoff of my terror campaign, aimed at getting the U.S. armed forces back home from Iraq. Over the next five months I have plans to bring seven plagues of fire and pestilence against the leaders of the government, based on the plagues that Moses used to get his people out of Egypt.

This first attack, while really just an early warning to Congress and the President of things to come, holds the most personal danger to me of all of my plans. The napalm I am about to unleash on the cars in the Congressional parking lot at Reagan National Airport has been loaded into an old mosquito sprayer I had stolen earlier tonight from a District of Columbia motor pool parking lot. The science says that the flash temperature of the napalm mix is high enough that it will not ignite from the heat of the sprayer's blower motor - but physics has been proven to be wrong at times in the past! I'm scared of starting the sprayer's motor, scared of what the future holds, but determined to heed God's call that I do something about the Americans dying in Iraq. So I hold my breath, close my eyes, and mutter a quick prayer.

Will my initial attacks change our government's policy toward the war? Probably not. But if the current administration doesn't want to bring our troops home, perhaps the replacements for the people I kill might be more amenable. In *The Fixer*, Bernard Malamud wrote about how people are more easily mobilized to action by their fears than their hopes. If I can get the public to fear my plagues enough, there may be a general outcry that will help get the withdrawal from Iraq moving more quickly.

God has given me this opportunity to help end an unjust war by putting me in the right place at the right time, with the skills I need and access to the resources necessary to pull off my plan. My mission became clear to me only three days after the government brought my dad home in a box. God revealed this opportunity just as we lowered my dad into the cold ground this past January. For six months I've planned, done reconnaissance, and put together my collection of toys and bugs. My dad was an Old Testament kind of guy, and he raised me the same way. Now it is time for some retribution. It has been tough to be patient, to wait until everything is prepared and in place. Now it is finally time to begin.

I'm starting with a fairly innocuous warning, and no one should get hurt in this attack. This is my version of the "thunder and hail and fire fell to the earth" plague discussed in Exodus, Chapter 8. Just some early 4th of July fireworks in our nation's capital. Or as Willie Shakespeare would have said if he had seen our Congress in action (or lack thereof), "A pox on both your houses." I pushed the sprayer's starter button.

Chapter 2

Bill Peterson
Peterson townhouse, Alexandria, VA
03:15 AM, Tuesday, July 4, 2006

I was lying in bed, dozing, and half-listening to the soft breathing of my wife. She's started sleeping on her back more now that she is expecting. We had the air conditioning going, because it had been a hot start to July in the D.C. area. All we had over us was a sheet and a light comforter, more like a security blanket than anything needed for warmth. I've determined that if you look closely enough, you can see the pattern from the bed comforter reflected on the ceiling, even if that reflection is just from the moonlight seeping through the window blinds.

Looking for ceiling patterns had gotten to be a habit lately. I haven't been sleeping well. Tonight it's either from the Chinese food we had for dinner, or else that feeling in my bones that something is about to break loose. I know that July 4th is a prime terrorist opportunity waiting to happen, and we in the FBI have seen the threat count from the Middle East ratcheting up recently. So I have reasons for not sleeping too soundly.

Most government employees (including both Julie and me) had taken Monday, July 3rd off too, to get a 4-day weekend. The two of us had spent most of our time off cleaning out an upstairs bedroom that had been our home office.

We are planning on making it into a nursery. Now that the 4th had actually arrived, I figured that if the country could make it through another 24 hours, we would be safely through the time period where some jihadist might think that an attack on the United States would make twisted sense as a way to get back at mom, apple pie, and the American way. We almost made it.

My first thought when my Blackberry's email alarm and cell phone chime both went off within 8 seconds of each other was that the COOP communications protocol actually did work, and that it was interesting that the email message had gotten through to me before the phone rang. My second was more down to earth - we had blown it, and terror was on the loose. We had failed again, for the first time since 9/11, and done so on my watch. As a team leader in the FBI's anti-terrorism task force, I'm senior enough now that I know when exercises have been scheduled, and this was no drill. If the Continuation of Operations Plan alarms were going off, somewhere terrorists had struck again at the United States and our citizens. I knew that both messages would be automated versions of "emergency - call your office," so I pulled the sheet off, swung my legs out of bed, and turned off the Blackberry ringers.

Julie stirred and mumbled, "I'll make some coffee," as I picked up the remote to click on CNN. They usually know well before anyone else about the latest crisis, and they are used as a source throughout the intelligence community - by both sides. I started getting dressed, and then the TV woke me up the rest of the way without me needing the cup of Columbia's best instant brew that my wife was bringing into our bedroom. Julie sat down beside me on the edge of the bed to watch with me. A long lens shot from the top of a CNN tower camera in Washington made it look like the entire Reagan National Airport was on fire. Scenarios and responses flashed through my mind as I speed dialed the situation room at our building on Pennsylvania Avenue. Terrorists? Attempted hijacking? Plane crash? Then CNN switched to a closer camera from the top of one of the taller parking garages at the airport, and I could see that the fire was in a parking area half the size of a football field, just southeast of the old terminal. It looked like every car in the lot was on fire.

Jack Simpson, the duty officer, answered the phone at FBI Headquarters. Seeing my ID on the screen, he didn't bother with pleasantries. "Bill, it looks like someone deliberately hit the parking lot reserved for members of Congress at National. We have a lot of cars on fire, and one major explosion just before the first airport fire truck arrived on the scene. From what the firemen are saying, the fires are very difficult to extinguish. One of the fire captains is a Vietnam vet, and he says that it looks like someone used napalm, or something just like it, to show their displeasure with Congress. You are already authorized to take charge of what is going to be a very messy crime scene. Homeland Security has already notified the Metro police, the Transportation Security Agency, and the Secret Service that we will be the lead agency on this one. I'll let your team know to meet you there as they call in."

I told him, "If you get anything new, call me. And Jack, if you hear from Tom, tell him I'm on the case." Just over a month ago, on June 1st, I had been promoted to lead an expert group of terrorist attack first responders. Tom Lawrence, currently out of town on vacation, was my new boss, so he needed to be in the loop. My team's job was to gather the evidence to convict someone or some group for the crime, and to develop ammunition that could help us to deter the next attempt at invading our shores. While Homeland Security has overall control of all security efforts in the United States, they always defer to the FBI when it gets to where the rubber meets the road. That's fine. We're damn good at what we do. The general public will never know how many attempts at terror we have stopped before they ever got close to succeeding. While we failed to stop this one before the attack, we will do our best to make sure this episode will not be repeated. So this case belonged to the Bureau. More specifically, it belonged to me and my team. I kissed Julie goodbye, and told her, "I'll call you later, when I can get a better handle on what's going on, and how long I'll be. You might as well go back to bed."

She said, "I'm already awake. I guess I'll stay up and start painting in the nursery. It's too bad you can't stay and help. I know how much you love to paint."

I laughed at that, and said, "Well, I guess if terrorists can strike on the 4th, we can catch them on the 4th." I headed out the door.

On the way in to the airport from my townhouse in Alexandria, I tried to get more info. I dropped the Blackberry into the hands-free speaker system in the Chevy Malibu assigned to me (tight on my 6-4 frame, but I was happy just to have gotten high enough in the food chain to be assigned a company car), and called Jack back. "Anything new?"

Jack said, "One of the Assistant Directors just stopped by the situation room, telling everyone there that The Bureau is already getting calls from screaming congressmen and senators, wanting to know what we are going to do to find the group that torched their cars, and that hearings would be scheduled as soon as they could get back to D.C. We really don't have much new on the situation at the airport. The Secret Service guys assigned there are asking if we need their assistance. Your entire team has checked in, and they are all meeting you at the scene."

Jack and I agreed that someone would be held accountable by Congress for allowing this to happen, and that we wouldn't want to be the FBI Director when he had to appear as a witness before the subcommittee assigned to investigate this. At this point, nothing had been released to say that this was more than a car fire that had gotten out of control - but everyone with a microphone, especially the TV people, were already speculating that this was another terrorist incident. Jack told me that we had people checking with news sources from the Post to Al Jazeera, but so far no notice claiming responsibility had been sent to anyone. All we would have would be the evidence we could develop. My team was well trained, and we love a challenge - but Jack was right about this one. It was going to be a mess.

As I turned onto the George Washington Parkway, and started fighting my way through the roadblocks already set up by the D.C. police to keep the curious (and quickly summoned congressional aides) out of the area, I got mad. Why did someone have to do this on my watch? Things had finally started going pretty well for Julie and me. We're both 36, and a little old to be having our first child. We've been together for 14 years, having met while I was in law school at The University of Texas, and she was working on her Masters at the Lyndon Johnson School of Public Affairs in Austin. We waited late to get married, and waited even later to have children. We both agreed that establishing our careers came first. I've had my tours of duty out in the field, in places like Milwaukee and Phoenix, before finally working my way up to ASAC in Chicago before my current gig. Now I was one step from the job I had coveted since I was in law school - Assistant Director for Counter Terrorism at the FBI. The AD job was the highest law enforcement position in the country that could be reached without becoming a political animal. I didn't want to run for election, or have to kiss enough asses to get appointed Director or Associate Director. The Assistant Director slot has been my goal, and terrorist attacks like this parking lot fiasco could either be an opportunity for me to shine, or a failure that would mean I never would get the job I had always wanted. "FBI Assistant Director Bill Peterson announced today the arrest of the alleged parking lot arsonist" sounds a whole lot better to me than "Ex-FBI Team Leader Bill Peterson was replaced today, after failing to solve the Congressional Parking Lot fire case."

I can remember having a little spare time in some of my past assignments. I used to take in an occasional spring training Cactus League baseball game, or a Cardinals football game, when I was in Phoenix. I even took some flying lessons in Milwaukee, getting good enough to solo and get my basic private pilot license. I wasn't ready to fly 747s, but I could get a small plane up and down, and had even considered buying a share in a plane with a few of my pilot buddies before I got promoted to Chicago. But from 9/11 on it has been full speed ahead, and there hasn't been time for fun and games. In fact, there hasn't been much time for Julie, either. I know she resents my workaholic ways, but she knew that about me when she married me. I know that unbridled ambition can sometimes hurt more than it helps, but there are bad guys out there that need catching, terrorist attacks that need preventing, and I want that AD job! Once I get where I want to be, there will hopefully be more time for my wife and family.

At the same time, Julie has been climbing the hierarchy at the State Department. She and Condi have gotten pretty tight. Julie is now a "Special Assistant to the Secretary of State," and Secretary Rice listens to the advice Julie gives her - which means that sometimes that advice goes all the way to the White House. As for the baby, we now feel we are as ready as we are ever going to be, considering that no one is ever really ready to be a parent. By the time I got to the airport, I was pretty pissed that someone had decided to start celebrating the 4th a little early - but at the same time realizing that this case could make my career.

Reagan National Airport
04:10 AM Tuesday, July 4, 2006

The airport scene was actually not total bedlam. I had expected to find things a lot worse than they really were. The airport fire department was still trying to get the fires out, but at least it looked like they were having some success. I introduced myself to their Chief, a guy named Parker, and asked how things were going.

He said, "We've discovered that the foam we had stored for aircraft fires also works to put out the gasoline mixture used on the cars out here. The only problem we're having now is that we're being forced to spray from a good distance back, because a couple of additional gas tanks have blown, sending shrapnel from cars all the way across the lot."

I asked, "How long until we can investigate the scene?"

"We're finally getting it under control. I would guess it will be another 45 minutes or so before the fires are completely out. After that, probably another hour or so to cool enough that it would be safe for your agents to enter the lot."

I told the Chief, "Thanks. Let me know when you get things the way you want them. I understand you have a job to do, and I don't want to interfere with that - but we need the lot as soon as you can clear it. And I would ask that you tell your people to try and preserve any potential evidence you find while putting this out. We are going to need all the help we can get to catch whoever pulled this."

He nodded, and I hoped he would leave the scene as untouched as possible. A lot of people don't like the FBI coming in and "taking over" - so we have to be careful not to step on someone's ego, if they have a chance to mess up our potential evidence. I know most fire people hate arsonists, too, and I felt like he would cooperate.

Then I started looking around for my team. I found where they had set up a temporary base just inside the doors to the old terminal. They had already asked that the airport police start evacuating what few employees were in the old terminal at that time of the morning, and had the police prepared to tape off the crime scene once the fires were out and the lot declared safe. Everyone was being moved to the new terminal, and the Red Cross was supposedly on the way with donuts and coffee. I didn't want to think about what this incident was going to do to 4th of July travel schedules for people planning on flying in or out of National! I made sure that no one was being allowed to leave before we could get an initial interview, and started making team assignments. My people knew what the drill was supposed to be, and really didn't need any direction from me. We had one guy off on vacation for the week, but everyone else was there and ready to go. Three of my guys went to start the interview process. Two stayed on the scene of the fire, to make sure nothing disturbed the crime scene any more than necessary.

I took Agent Sally Caruthers with me. She is my security expert, and we went to find whoever was in charge of the airport security team. Sally is an interesting story. She is 26, and one of the youngest FBI agents ever. She was a child genius, going to college at the age of 13, and graduating from Georgetown Law at 18. Her gift for knowing how to make computers do back flips got her a job at the National Security Agency, and she worked there until she was 21. After 9/11, when the FBI announced we were expanding our agent base, and one of the specialties we were looking for was Information Technology, she applied for an agent position. She did not meet the eligibility requirements to apply, because she wasn't 23. But the Director waived that requirement for her, because of the special circumstances of her skill level and experience. The NSA screamed, but our Director was happy that she wanted to join us.

Everyone that knew of the situation assumed that she would end up in our computer lab, but she really just wanted to be an agent on the street. No one thought she had much of a chance of making it through the academy, but she finished at the top of her class. She may not have much experience on the street, but brains can make up for a lot. She doesn't miss much when working a crime, and I'm happy to have her on my team. She knows more about security techniques than anybody this side of the Mossad, the Israeli spy agency.

We found the airport security office behind a one way glass mirror looking down at the ticket area in the new terminal. The office looked a little odd when we walked in, and I realized that was because so many of the monitors on the wall showed no activity - all of the old terminal, and major sections of the new terminal had been evacuated. A couple of the National Airport Secret Service people, the ones permanently stationed at National, were already in the security office. I knew one of the agents.

"Hi, Bill," said agent Arnie Ross. "This one dumped on you? Sure looks like someone wanted to roast Congress!" I groaned. He filled me in on what they knew, which wasn't much more than what we already had. Ross told me that George O'Leary, the captain in charge of airport security on the swing shift, was of course off for the holiday, and vacationing down at Virginia Beach. His replacement was Lt. Sam Hardesty, and he was already reviewing the tapes of the airport areas we wanted to see with the Secret Service people. We got through the introductions, and started watching what Hardesty had already cued up on his VCR. Most people don't know how well D.C. is wired these days. Thanks to inexpensive web cams, and the nice budget given to Homeland Security, it was hard to sneeze outdoors or anywhere around one of the major monuments or museums in Washington without someone half way across town saying, "Gesundheit!" We knew we would have the terrorists on video tape or DVD, and probably from several different cameras across the area.

Hardesty's first tape, taken from a camera directly over the parking lot entrance, showed a pickup pulling a trailer driving up to the gate for the parking lot, a gloved hand coming out the window of the pickup sliding a card into the slot used to open the gate, and the pickup and trailer quickly bouncing over the gate rail as they entered the lot. Sam had a second tape, taken from the corner of the old terminal, showing the driver of the pickup getting out of the truck in the lot, cranking up what looked like a big health department mosquito sprayer on the trailer, and then driving around the parking lot with the sprayer running, spraying the entire area. There wasn't much wind, and it was shifting directions, so the spray wasn't traveling more than 15 - 20 feet before settling. It might have looked like he was fogging for mosquitoes, but we knew it wasn't repellant in the trailer.

Sally said, "I timed it. He covered the entire lot in 6 minutes, 10 seconds."

The tape showed the guy leaving the pickup and trailer in the middle of the parking lot, walking to the terminal entry gate, and pulling something out of his pocket (the tape quality was not that good).

Arnie, said, "What is that, a flashlight?"

Lt. Hardesty said, "Too thick for a flashlight. Must be some sort of igniter for the Napalm."

We discovered that he was right - the "flashlight" was a small portable welding torch.

We knew when our terrorist lit the torch, and we could see the bright flame. He focused the nozzle on the torch to get the flame as hot as possible, and then touched the blue flame to the gasoline compound he had sprayed on the cars in the lot. He started on an SUV, the one parked nearest to the walkway entrance. I had seen that same vehicle this morning when I was at the parking lot, and what used to be a Lincoln Navigator now looked like burned toast.

Arnie snorted. I looked up at him, and he said, "Someone thought they had lucked into a great parking space."

I couldn't help but grin while we watched more of the tape. The flames spread quickly. Gasoline does tend to feed a fire well.

Sally asked, "Why didn't the gas ignite in the sprayer? Wouldn't that motor be hot enough to ignite the gas fumes?"

I told her, "Good question, and I don't know. We'll follow up on that one." She made a note.

Within a couple of minutes a good part of the lot was in flames, and then came a tremendous explosion, when the fire found the remaining gas and fume mix in the trailer's reservoir. That ended the video from the camera we were watching. I don't know if the explosion destroyed the camera, melted the power source, or if something actually struck the lens on the camera, but that was the finale of the show.

We did get some low light pictures of the guy from the video. Sally said, "Tell me if you agree with what I've got. I say about 5-10 or 5-11, thin, wearing what looked like a maintenance uniform of some sort. He was wearing gloves, tennis shoes, and a baseball cap. He had to know that he was going to be on film, because he was also wearing a Spiderman mask. Did anyone pick up anything I missed on Spidey?"

No one had anything to add. We had no way of knowing what he looked like at all, unless our forensic people back at the lab could do something with shapes from the mask. Not likely with the quality of the tapes, but we could always hope.

I said, "What we don't have from this view is film of the jerk leaving the scene. Did he get picked up by an accomplice, walk away, or have some other form of transportation available? It's only a few hundred yards to the Metro entrance, but I doubt that he stood around waiting for the next train at that time of the morning."

Sally added, "Or did he leave at all? Was he an airport employee, or was he mixed in with the people we had gathered from the two terminals? Was he alone, or were there others involved? At this point we have to consider every option."

The main road at the airport runs in a big circle, coming from the parking garage areas, circling around in front of the terminals, and then moving back towards the Parkway. Unless the

26

unsub had fled on foot, or gone the wrong way on the road back toward the parking garages, he had to have come by the terminal - and cameras monitor that area, too. I asked Sam to run the film for the terminal roadway for the 5 to 10 minutes after the fire was set. The first film showed nothing moved during that time in the pickup area in front of the terminal.

The tape for the drop off area showed one car driving up and stopping, dropping off a guy in an airline uniform. That made me think it was probably an employee, but I asked Sally to check to see if we could identify that guy, and if he saw anything at the Congressional lot entrance. After about a 5 minute break without any vehicles coming through, someone came by on a Harley motorcycle.

"Stop it there and zoom in on the cyclist," I asked.

It was obviously our guy, even down to the same gloves, but now he wore a motorcycle helmet over his mask. We knew how he had gotten out of the airport area. Now we just had to catch him. We got an APB out, along with stills taken from the tapes, but I didn't have much faith in anyone spotting him. By this time he had over a 90 minute head start, and my gut feeling was that he was long gone. We assigned people to watch the camera feeds from all the major roads in real time, just to see if we could spot him. We even put the info out on the AMBER Alert system, just in case an early holiday commuter might find himself behind that particular motorcycle out on the Beltway. I wasn't holding my breath.

FBI Headquarters
12:08 PM, Tuesday, July 4, 2006

Contrary to popular belief, the FBI isn't like the Canadian Mounties - we don't always get our man. But we are damn good at throwing manpower at every possible lead, and building a case as quickly as possible. We do catch a lot more of the bad guys than we miss, although some do manage to slip through our nets, at least for a while. We now knew a lot more than we did at five AM, considering that we are short resources on the holiday, and still trying to find people to come in and help. We still had no announcement as to why the attack, but we had developed a lot of information on how the operation was carried out. We found the motorcycle in the Potomac, just off shore in Lady Bird Johnson Park - just a mile or so outside the airport. Some early joggers in the park spotted the gleam in the water, and called it in after our AMBER alert. The bike was stolen late Monday evening in Arlington, but not missed until Tuesday morning. Apparently our boy rode the bike from Arlington into D.C., to the municipal Health Department motor pool lot on North St NE, and cut the chain on the gate at that lot. He then proceeded to load the bike into the back of a D.C. Health Department pickup truck, hotwire the truck, hook up an old mosquito sprayer onto the trailer ball on the truck, and pull out of the lot.

We have him on film driving by the Kennedy Center on his way to the airport, with the pickup pulling the trailer. We know that he stopped somewhere between the Health Department and the airport and loaded the mosquito sprayer with gasoline, kerosene, and polystyrene, which makes a homemade Napalm-B type mixture. We haven't been able to determine where he did the trailer filling, but we are working on it. And somehow he managed to get that stuff mixed in the trailer, forming a slurry. We know our boy is smart - our follow up on why the sprayer didn't explode showed that if he had used just gasoline, the heat from the engine on the sprayer would have ignited the gas. However, the gas/polystyrene slurry requires a much higher temperature for ignition compared to gasoline, and therefore was safe to be run through the sprayer fan with the sprayer engine running. The higher ignition temperature required by Napalm is why he used his welding torch to start the fire.

It is stupid that the sprayer was available to be stolen. Our *uber*-liberal friends that run D.C. are too afraid to spray for mosquitoes, since there is a slight chance that the spray might kill off the Hays Spring Amphipod (whatever that is) in Rock Creek Park, or some diplomat from Lower Slobovia might get upset if a little insecticide spray drifted into the back yard of his sacrosanct embassy. The D.C. Health Department's practice

29

is to wait until the West Nile Virus shows up in some mosquito test trap, or some animal or human comes down with the disease, and then go around and put insecticide in standing pools of water in that area of town – but no spraying. Talk about shutting the barn door after the cows get out! So who knows why the D.C. Health Department still had a sprayer sitting in their motor pool parking lot? Apparently they had finally decided to get rid of it, and listed it on the Internet as available for sale. They hadn't had any nibbles on the attempted sale, and it was probably too much trouble to try and dump it on some other area municipality, so it just sat - until our guy put it to use last night. He might have even discovered it was available because of the online listing.

We don't know how he got to Arlington to steal the bike, and we don't know how he left LBJ Park, or which direction he went from that point. We don't know why he did what he did. This was obviously too well planned to just be some teenager's prank. We've made some progress, but we need to know more if we're going to get this guy. At least at this point we seem to have come to the conclusion that it was just one guy, and not an entire cell. He may have had some help, but we can't see where, other than possibly with the trailer loading and mixing. Most of my team agrees that it looks like one guy seems to have pulled this one off all on his own.

Sally brought us tuna sandwiches wrapped in cellophane from the cafeteria in the basement, and while we ate we started going over what we now knew, and what we had missed. Sally is perky cute, and I catch her every now and then looking at me with those big brown eyes like a puppy waiting for a dog bone. I thought for a while that she had a little crush on me (or that may just be my ego and imagination getting carried away), but now I think we have settled into more of a mentor/student relationship. I know that I am married with a pregnant wife at home, and messing around with the company help is a good way to end up on the street, or chasing bank robbers in Juneau - but sometimes when I see Sally looking at me, it's hard to remember the new rules about harassment. I'm trying to stay focused on the case.

She brought up a point I had missed - where did our guy get the pass card to get in the gate? She called the airport security office, to see if their system recorded the number on the card and the time of entry. Sam was gone, but the guy on duty looked it up, and said the card belonged to Congressman Eric Coleman, a first term Democrat from Mississippi. The file report on the missing card said that he had reported losing his card back in May, and had been issued a duplicate. The report said that Coleman claimed that he always left his card in his car, but when he went to use it to park the car at the airport when he was going home for the Memorial Day weekend, the card had disappeared. This told us something new - that our perp had been planning this operation for months.

But it also brought up a new question. How did our guy know that Coleman kept his card stored in his car? The computer records showed that Coleman had used his original card to park in the lot on the Friday before Easter, back in April, so his card had been stolen sometime during April or May. Kicking the stolen card idea around, the team came up with a couple of additional assumptions. One, that our guy had somehow been watching cars coming into the lot, and probably on that Friday when Coleman had last used his original card. Since someone sitting on the public parking garage roof, where the rental cars are stored, and using binoculars to watch the Congressional Parking lot would have stood out as a possible threat to the TSA people, we came to the conclusion that our guy had mounted his own web cam or small video camera somewhere near the Congressional Parking Lot, with a view of people approaching the badge reader that opened the gate.

The second assumption was that all he had to have was a computer within a mile or so of that web cam to record everyone coming into the lot, and what they did with their cards after they used them to open the gate. He could have left a car in one of the parking garages for that weekend, ridden the shuttle to the terminal, and then walked to the metro for his trip back home.

Or he could have rented a hotel room at one of the hotels near the airport, and recorded everything shown on the web cam from the comfort of his room. He then stole the card from the car, either that weekend while the car was in the lot, or more probably at a later date.

I was leaning more toward the web cam and the parked car in the airport garage idea. I didn't think he would want to be using a credit card at a hotel, and leaving that trail, and he would show up on the hotel's video when he checked in. Web cams are pretty small, and could have been easily hidden where it could have seen what was happening at the gate, and no one had spotted the camera back in the spring.

Hoping against hope, we called the airport security office for tapes of the garages from the April/Easter weekend time frame, to try and get a list of the cars that were using one of the garages during that period, but the security office was still using one of the old video systems where the tapes were recycled every month. They only had 31 tapes, and replaced the tape daily with the tape with the same date from the previous month. The new digital recorders could store months of data, but no one had imagined that the garage tapes would be critical evidence months after the fact. I couldn't blame them for not having switched out the recorders - even the Transportation Security Administration has a budget, and all of us working for Uncle Sam understand how dry that wishing well can be when you ask for something that is not an absolute necessity - and you can't tag every item as a "National Security issue," especially with us spending billions in Iraq.

We sent people out to check the rosters (and get registration video tapes, if available) for every hotel within web cam broadcasting distance, but it was my personal opinion that we were just spinning our wheels at this point. As I said, we needed more if we were going to solve this one. Time to go upstairs, and make my report. The brass is not going to like hearing how little we know. And Congress is going to like it even less.

My boss, Assistant Director for Counterterrorism Thomas Lawrence, had made it back for this first case brief. He rode back down the elevator with me after I had gone over the facts and our conjectures with the powers that be. My first impression of him is that he might be a nice guy to sit and talk with over a beer after work, but at work he is something else. His favorite saying is that, "it's not personal - it's just business." In other words, he doesn't care if you are his favorite person in the Bureau. Either you get the job done, or you will not be working for Tom. Unfortunately, according to the stories I have been hearing, he has a reputation for micromanaging every team under his control. I have been told by my fellow team leaders that he is always making "suggestions" that the team leaders ignore at their own peril. They tell me that he is also bad about chewing out his team leaders in front of their peers - not the greatest in management techniques, if you want to build loyalty and high morale amongst the staff. This is obviously not the best working situation I have ever been in, but you have to take the boss that comes with the promotion. I hadn't worked for him long enough to form my own opinion of him, but I am wary. He told me in the elevator that he wanted to know every detail about how we planned to track this guy down, so I invited him to come back to my office for the resumption of our team meeting.

I thought he might just stand in a corner, but he took the spot right in front of my desk, and leaned back against the desk - where I was going to stand. I moved to a chair off to one side. He started off saying, "I'm just here to observe. It is Bill's meeting, and I don't want any of you to feel shy with me here. If you have any ideas, speak up. Congress is going to be on our butts, and we need to get this one solved fast."

Sally was sitting next to me, and I heard her mutter, "Yeah, right," so softly that no one else heard her.

We kicked around what else we could do. Andy brought up checking area hotels with the description info and time window we had on approximately when our perp might have returned to his room after the attack. Some hotels do track the times that door locks are accessed for each room, and we could check and see who opened their door from the outside for the time period in question. Not that many people are going back into their rooms at 5 or 6 in the morning on a holiday. Sally said that we should get people reviewing video tapes for people headed on the Metro to Arlington Monday evening. Our perp had to get there somehow, before he could steal the motorcycle. I added to the list that we needed taxi drop off info for anyone ending a ride near where the motorcycle was stolen. We also needed to check Arlington bus videos, metro videos in both Arlington and around the LBJ park area, and to see if any taxis reported pickups out of LBJ Park or the surrounding area early this morning. We needed our lab to tell us from the unburned gas sample from the lot what brand of gasoline was used, so that we could start tracking down the source. It wasn't much of a plan, but we didn't have much information to use as a base to build on. Mr. Lawrence didn't seem impressed. His comments made me feel that he was looking at us as a glorified CSI team. He seems to think that we are here to investigate the crime, and come up with the clues to get an indictment. I was told when I interviewed for the job (with Executive Assistant Director Willie Hulon, who is Lawrence's boss) that the team was designed to get ahead of the bad guys, anticipate what they were planning to do next, and get there first and stop them. I'm not sure Lawrence is on the same page as Mr. Hulon. I don't want to start my first big case arguing with my boss, but we are more than evidence gatherers. While we are going to be the team that catches this guy, we also want to make sure there are no additional attacks. Somehow, we may have to get around Lawrence to make that happen, but catching bad guys and stopping terrorist attacks are my first priorities. I think if we manage that we will keep Lawrence happy, too.

Robert Smithson
Journal Entry
Tuesday, July 4, 2006

I had two worries as I drove into the Congressional lot early this morning. The first was would the sprayer start? The ad on the Internet advertising the sprayer for sale said that it was in working condition. The battery was fully charged when I checked it. But would it actually crank when I hit the starter switch? The second question was even more critical - when the fuel mix was heated before it hit the sprayer fan would I end up disappearing in one big flash as the whole thing exploded? The science theory was sound, saying that the ignition temperature of the slurry I was using was high enough that it should spray without igniting as it went through the sprayer. However, sometimes theories don't prove to be true - that's why they are called theories. When the motor cranked, and the spray actually started blowing through the fan, I knew that I was on my way to getting our troops home.

It would be a winding road, but every journey starts with the first step. Me spouting platitudes? Can you tell I was more than a tad nervous? Sometimes prayers are answered when you are scared shitless!

The results were actually better than I expected. A whole bunch of vehicles were burning pretty fiercely when I walked out of the parking lot through the passenger gate. I had taken the motorcycle out of the bed of the pickup before I pulled into the lot, because I didn't want to take any chances on not being able to get to it when I started the fire. So when I kick started the bike, I had a nice satisfied feeling of accomplishment. Not a bad effort for a first attempt, and I was actually pretty proud of myself. I had developed a plan, carried it off, and it looked like I was going to be able to get away with it. Unfortunately, I couldn't brag to anyone about what I had accomplished!

I had found the sprayer when the D.C. Health Department listed it as surplus equipment on the Internet, trying to get rid of it. The formula for homemade Napalm-B was available online, and it only took me about 15 seconds to find it. You can probably get the instructions for building a nuclear missile if you want them off the Internet - anything and everything is available with today's search engines. I take the credit for putting the giant flamethrower idea together, but it probably will not take long before the idea is uploaded onto the net so as to be available for the next would-be crusader.

Stealing a pass card to the parking lot gate was not that difficult, either. I had my choice of 3 different Congressmen that my web cam video picked up leaving their airport gate access cards in their cars in April when they opened the National parking lot gate, so I had to get their D.C. addresses and check out each of them. While watching Coleman's place I found that he parked in an underground garage beneath his apartment complex, so his was the easiest car to get access to - no personal garage or building locks to bother with. Back in early May, I drove into his parking area right behind a car that had a pass to his apartment's garage, and stayed in my rental car until the people ahead of me had gotten on the elevator. I took a long stick and jiggled the security camera in his lot, so that it pointed up instead of down, and I used a Slim Jim to pop his car door lock. I was in and out of his parking lot within 5 minutes, and relocked his car so that he wouldn't likely notice that it had been burglarized. My only question then was whether or not that old card would be deactivated after he was issued a new card, so I had to wait until he left town again, and was issued a new gate card. I tried the old card in June, and it let me into the lot without a problem. I took down my web cam from the light post across the street from the parking lot gate at the same time. You would think that security people would think about risks like this, but I guess parking lots are not considered to be high security areas. They might change their procedures on deactivating old cards after this soiree!

I knew security would be light at two AM in the morning at the airport. Flights don't start taking off and landing there until around six AM, so that the neighbors living close to the airport can get a little sleep. I had watched on my web cam how many times a patrol car drove by, and it was only about once per hour that time of night on a regular weeknight, and I was expecting even less security coverage on a holiday. I wasn't too worried about being interrupted while spraying. I realized that I would end up on video, so I wore the mask. The lot was packed full - lots of members of Congress apparently went home for the 4th weekend. The ones that stayed in D.C. probably loaned their parking lot cards to some staffer that was flying home. I didn't bother to count how many donkey or elephant decals I saw. For this particular exercise, I really didn't care which political party I hit. I wanted all of Congress to suffer for following behind Bush and Cheney like a puppy on a leash!

After leaving the airport, I dumped the bike in the river as it flowed by the park, and waded in and took the rocks out of the square-tailed canoe that I had hidden there earlier, allowing it to refloat. I pulled the battery and electric boat motor out of the bushes, installed them on the canoe, cranked up the 3 HP battery powered motor, and ran upstream for about a mile to the first bridge. The water was peaceful and quiet at that time of the morning. The tide was pretty slack, there wasn't much wind, and I was the only boat moving on the water. The battery powered motor barely made any noise at all. I hoped that my canoe's bow wave was a sign, showing that my planned attacks would spread my opinion of the war to the rest of the country, just like my wave was spreading to each shoreline.

I sank the portable welder, the mask, and the bike helmet in the middle of the river as I approached the bridge. There are usually homeless staying under the bridge where I wanted to disembark, but the D.C. and park police had cleared out the bums for the 4th weekend, to keep the tourists from being hassled for spare change while they visited the monuments and museums. I pushed the canoe back into the river and left it floating back downriver. I was certain that it would be stolen again before any cop found it. I had kept my gloves on while I was using the canoe, so I didn't leave any fingerprints in it, just in case. I changed shirts and caps under the bridge, walked up to the street, and I became just another jogger with a backpack, out for my morning exercise. It was only about a mile to the nearest metro station. Within an hour I was riding the first train on the yellow line back to my hotel in Bethesda, and by 6:30 I was watching the fire at the airport on TV. There are enough people, even on a holiday, riding the Metro at 6 AM that I wasn't worried about standing out and being identified as someone fleeing the airport.

I did screw up in one minor way. I didn't get into the Washington metro area until late on Sunday, driving up from North Carolina. God, I hate bureaucracy. It's bad enough that I have to deal with this country's incompetent administration, but to deal with the administration of my university, too? It's enough to make a man crazy. As a biochemistry grad student at The University of North Carolina, I have to jump through the necessary hurdles of my degree program so that I can get access to the necessary reagents and equipment that I need for executing my plans. I regularly show up in the lab and look like I'm working hard on my PhD research project on the genomics of pathogenic viruses, even if all I am really doing is preparing for the plagues I am going to unleash on our political elite. I had worked late Saturday in the lab running an experiment, so I couldn't get to Washington before late Sunday evening. So even though I had preprinted the warning messages, and prepared the envelopes going to the Post, the NY Times, a couple of the local TV stations, and the various politicians and groups I am targeting, I didn't get them in the mail until Monday. What I didn't realize is that there is no mail delivery on July 4th, even to the news groups with PO Boxes. My warning would not be announced to the world until Wednesday, July 5th. Considering that I did not want heightened security while I sprayed and played "Light My Fire," perhaps it was for the best that they will receive my warning after the fact. I'll consider that in my future planning.

One of the hardest parts of this campaign was determining what to say. I wanted the warning to be taken seriously, even though I know that the initial warning would not be enough to get the pull-out process started. For the people I am targeting, oil prices and profits are much more important than some homegrown terrorist telling them they need to shape up and start shipping people out of Iraq. While the Bible talks about ten plagues brought against the Egyptians, I am going to skip a few. I could do gnats and flies (some biblical translations seem to think lice were used) if I had to, but they would be more of a nuisance in today's society than a dangerous plague. Locusts would be even more of a problem to release in plague proportions, not to mention the time it would take to go to the Midwest to catch a swarm, or the time it would take to raise my own. I didn't want to say that there would just be seven attacks, to match seven of the plagues from Moses' day. I didn't want them anticipating a certain number of attacks, or else trying to wait out all seven. I finally came up with something direct and simple for the first message, while still leaving the ideas I was trying to get across fairly generic:

A WARNING TO THE COUNTRY'S POLITICAL LEADERSHIP

FIND A WAY TO PULL THE AMERICAN TROOPS OUT OF IRAQ, OR YOU WILL PAY. EITHER YOU FIND A WAY, OR ELSE THE PEOPLE THAT REPLACE YOU WILL GET A CHANCE. AMERICANS ARE DYING IN VAIN IN THE MIDDLE EAST. EITHER YOU GET THEM OUT, OR YOUR ODDS OF SURVIVAL WILL BE WORSE THAN THE PEOPLE YOU HAVE SENT INTO HARM'S WAY. START YOUR EFFORTS NOW. YOU HAVE UNTIL THE END OF THIS CONGRESSIONAL TERM TO BEGIN THE PULL BACK PROCESS. SUPPORT THE IMMEDIATE RETURN HOME OF THE COALITION ARMED FORCES, AND YOU WILL NOT BE TARGETED. DO NOT TAKE THIS WARNING AS JUST

44

ANOTHER CRANK THREAT. JUST AS GOD BROUGHT THUNDER AND LIGHTNING AND FIRE AGAINST THE EGYPTIANS TO HELP FREE THE ISRAELITES FROM SLAVERY, THE SAME PLAGUE HAS BEEN BROUGHT AGAINST THE VEHICLES OF THOSE THAT SUPPORT THE WAR. WEAPONS OF MASS DESTRUCTION ARE AVAILABLE AND WILL BE USED IF NECESSARY. THE FIRE AT THE AIRPORT WAS THE FIRST WARNING, TO SHOW HOW SERIOUSLY YOU SHOULD TAKE THIS DEMAND. AS MOSES SAID TO THE EGYPTIANS, "LET MY PEOPLE GO!" IF PROGRESS IS NOT SEEN RAPIDLY, MORE PLAGUES AND PESTILENCE WILL RAIN DOWN UPON YOU, JUST AS DISCUSSED IN

THE BOOK OF EXODUS. START THINGS MOVING TOWARD TOTAL WITHDRAWAL, OR YOUR DAYS ARE NUMBERED!

Every time I think about getting the rest of our soldiers and marines home, my dad comes to mind. I have to keep reminding myself that getting even is better than getting mad. If I get too maudlin over my dad's death, I won't be able to concentrate on the tasks at hand. My mom hasn't been off of pills since they brought my dad home, and she will probably not last out the year. My sister cries every time she calls me. I want to tell her what I am going to do, but she wouldn't understand. Not too many people will, but this is another case where the end justifies the means. I can't save my family, but maybe I can make a difference for others, before it is too late for them, too.

The shock I felt when I got the phone call from my sister, telling me that our dad was dead, is something I will never get over. He has always been my rock, the steady point that I revolved around as I grew from a boy to the man I am today. I can't stand that the vault inside of me, where I kept my memories of him, grows emptier every day. Every time I try and pull up a specific look, day, or time we had together, I find that it is more difficult to remember the details. He made me who I am, and I'm doing this because of who I want to be. Am I mentally disturbed? Of course! There is no question. But I still have a genius level IQ, a great lab I can use to create weapons, and as Mary Stuart, Queen of Scots, put in back in the 16th century, "No more tears now; I will think upon revenge."

My dad deserves to be remembered as more than just another statistic. If I can use his death to help move things in the right direction, then maybe his death will not be in vain after all. My dad was quite the hero. Remember John Wayne in the old movie, "The Green Berets?" My dad made John Wayne look like a wimp. Lt. Colonel Robert Smithson was not only the greatest father in the world, but one of the leaders of Delta Force at Fort Bragg. We were not supposed to know that Dad was part of Delta, but the stuff he didn't say about what he was doing told us more than the little things he could tell us. He used to take Green Beret A-teams out into the swamps down at Eglin Air Force Base in the Florida panhandle, and work them over until even the meanest and most stubborn green beanies would admit that Delta did it better. He would use those war games in the swamp to help choose those he wanted to recruit for his team. He only chose the "best of the best," from both the Rangers and the Berets, and that was the credo of the entire Delta community.

The "Delta kids," those of us being raised on Bragg, were all expected to perform to a higher standard, too. We had great role models, and we subconsciously knew that giving less than our best would be disappointing to our parents. They were out there on the cutting edge, risking their lives on a regular basis to keep us free. We wanted them to be as proud of us as we were of them. Those of us with family working in the old stockade on Bragg knew what was going on there, even if we never discussed it with anyone else. It was fun being a kid on that base. Growing up around the Rangers and Delta Force made for some interesting times. For example, the Boy Scouts at Bragg were taught more than knot tying. We learned how to operate in a hostile urban environment, as well as how to do survival camping in the snow and ice in the Smokey Mountains. Even our games were a little more intense than what you would find with the usual group of 12-year-old boys playing "capture the flag." I know how to reconnoiter before an op, how to plan diversions and alternate escape scenarios, how to hotwire a vehicle, use disguises, and just as importantly, how to avoid leaving clues for the cops.

And as I alluded to in this journal earlier, I am also blessed to have the formal education and lab experience necessary to make a difference in this attempt to change our government's foreign policy toward the Middle East. As a biochemistry PhD candidate researching infectious diseases at a major research university, I know how to work with (and more importantly, have access to) the various bugs and toxins that the government is afraid might be used against us by terrorists. I also know I have to be careful, if I want to pull this off. I know the story of the anthrax attacks in the United States back in 2001, and I know that the FBI is 98% sure who did it - but they and the Postal Inspectors can't get the U.S. Attorney in Northern Virginia to issue an indictment, because the prosecuting attorney doesn't think he has enough evidence to get a conviction. I don't plan to get even that close to getting caught. For example, I am not going to use pre-existing weapon-grade Anthrax, because all of those cultures now have imbedded biological tracers that can be tracked back to a particular lab.

I am writing this journal, so if something does go radically wrong, there will be a record of exactly what I am doing, and why. As I mentioned earlier, there will be collateral damage during my attacks (especially this next one), and the families of those that do not survive my plagues deserve to know that their loved ones died for a greater cause. I know that is exactly what they said about my dad, but since we have no business being in Iraq, in his case that lie will not fly. If the FBI gets too close, I have taken a couple of extra precautions, which will hopefully give me enough time to complete my quest. I feel a little like Don Quixote - but I plan on bringing this windmill all the way down.

I know the difference between right and wrong, and I know that in some ways what I am doing is wrong. But I inherited more than my dad's name (I've dropped the "Junior.") I also have his stubborn streak, and a sense of the big picture that will allow me to take the actions I'm going to take. Some innocent people will get caught up in this mess, and I will feel sorry for them. But if that is what it takes to get our troops home, so be it. I have the courage to do what has to be done.

My quotient of bravery was put to the test last week. I knew that with this campaign starting, I didn't need complications in my life. So I knew that I had to break off my engagement to a wonderful lady here in Chapel Hill. We have been engaged for about six months, since last Christmas, just before my Dad was killed. She tried to help me to get over my dad's death, but nothing seemed to help that pain. Lisa is a great girl - loving, nurturing, funny, and beautiful. But I knew that eventually the FBI would discover who was behind the attacks, that my identity would be made public, and I didn't want her to be stained because of her relationship to me. Plus, as much as I was going to be running around the country the next few months, I knew that she might match my absences with the attacks on our government, and I didn't want her coming to conclusions that might end up with the FBI being notified.

I did and still do love that girl, but my mission is more important to me than anything, or anyone, right at this moment. So I had to lie. I told her that I had changed my mind, that I didn't want to get married, and that I didn't want to see her any more. I told her she could keep or sell the ring I had given her - I didn't want it back. I told her that there wasn't anyone else in my life, but that I was just not ready to settle down. It hurt me deeply to see her crying, but I knew that breaking up with her was really the best thing for her. She looked at me like I was crazy, and I couldn't tell her that maybe she was right. My new mistress was a cause, and not another woman. I felt like a traitor just the same.

And as Patrick Henry so aptly put it a couple of centuries ago, "If this be treason, make the most of it." He did end up apologizing for that speech in the House of Burgesses, because it implied (taken in context) that he was advocating the assassination of George III. I am taking that a step further, and not apologizing. If our leaders will not listen to the voice of the people, and there is no question that the majority of Americans want our troops out of Iraq, then those leaders need to be replaced by whatever means necessary. We can't wait for a slow ground swell to push the political process forward - by that time too many more unnecessary deaths will have occurred, and too many more families here in America will have had their lives ruined. I'm going to fix the problem one way or another, and do so within the next few months.

And speaking of why we are in Iraq, there is a part of the government that tried to convince the President and his kitchen cabinet that an attack on Baghdad and Hussein was necessary, because of the bio and nuclear weapons he was allegedly developing. I also read a report recently from people putting together Continuity of Operations (COOP) Plans for the government, saying that there were no provisions or plans in place for handling a pandemic in the D.C. area. The complaint in the report was that there was not enough bandwidth available for everyone to work on their computers from home. So if people couldn't get to work because of widespread illness problems, the government would have serious problems coping with the day to day minutia that is necessary to keep the government functioning. So what would happen if no one showed up at a government agency? Would the rest of the government find out that they could manage quite well without input from that agency? Hopefully we will find out in few weeks - and I will make sure my second warning gets out in a more timely fashion! Moses' first plague, trying to get the Pharaoh's attention, was turning water into blood. I can't do that miracle, but I can make taking a drink of water a chancy proposition...

Bill Peterson
FBI HQ
2:00 PM, Wednesday, July 5, 2006

We're getting there. We now have the threat message, warning us of further actions if the government doesn't pull our troops out of Iraq.

We have what we think is every copy - and copies went to the President, the Vice President, the Secretaries of State and Defense, leaders of both houses of Congress (a little late in my opinion), the CIA, and various media outlets. Even my big boss, Director Mueller, was sent what appears to be a courtesy copy! We're obviously checking all the letters and envelopes for DNA and fingerprints, and we can work with the message itself through our shrinks to get a psychological profile of this turkey. We also have a possible match on a web cam shot of the guy going down the escalator into a downtown Metro station early yesterday morning. The computers say the body sizes match, but we don't have a good shot of his face - at least not enough to use for identification. He kept his baseball cap on tight, and his head down at all times. We will be putting people on all the trains going through that station tomorrow morning, doing interviews to see if anyone remembers the guy on their train on the 4th.

Don Imus started calling this guy "Moses II," on his show this morning, after the wording in the warning message hit the news, and the rest of the media has now picked up that misnomer. The radical press is going wild, claiming that the rich elitist bastards in Congress deserved the fire, just for having the gall to still be using a parking lot reserved for their use alone. The White House has not issued an official statement, but the President's press secretary, Tony Snow, made the usual noises about how "we don't negotiate with terrorists." No luck on our inquiries on how the guy got to Arlington, and no luck at any D.C. area hotels. This guy could have been staying in Baltimore for all we know.

I sent a couple of team members back to the crime scene at the airport and search for hidden cameras, but we didn't find anything. We did discover that the stolen parking lot access card had been used in June, but the Congressman told us that it wasn't him - so it had to be our guy testing the card. We had video showing that the car that entered the lot in June was a dark blue Toyota Camry, probably a 2006 model, but no license plate numbers. There was no tape of the exit to the lot, so all we knew was that our perp had tried out his stolen card a month before the arson attack. We started working on building a database of Camry owners from around the country, and checking to see what rental agencies had Toyotas in their fleet being rented in this area during that timeframe.

We don't know for sure what the unsub, our "unknown subject," means by "let my people go." Is he an American, saying his people are the soldiers he wants out of the Middle East, or is he Iraqi, saying to get the oppressors out of his country, freeing the native population to solve their own problems? Half of our team is leaning toward an American, and half seem to think this is an Iraqi, or a front for an Iraqi/Middle Eastern cell. Our Behavioral Psychology Group says this guy seems to be seriously motivated, and that we should be prepared for additional activity from this turkey. His mention of WMDs has us all worried - we don't think an individual could get access to or build a nuke, but a biological weapon or a dirty bomb is always possible.

And now the pressure will start to build. Tom has been in my office 6 times today - I've seen more of him today than I have since I got the job. I've gotten five hours of sleep in the last 48 hours, and that was before my phone started ringing the morning of the 4th. Julie says she understands, but I know she misses me. The questions have already begun - from the press, from Congress, from the public. When can we expect an arrest? What can we do to stop this nutjob from attacking again? Where will he strike next? When will the next attack come? Nothing affects the American psyche more than *not knowing.* We have gotten too used to every bit of information we need being available when we need it. Not knowing something eats at us. Frustration sets in, and soon someone will suggest we need to start doing strip searches of everyone within 5 miles of the Washington Monument. If we let the terrorists take away too much of our freedom, then they win that way, too. The obvious solution is to catch this guy, and fast. Unfortunately, that is looking like it will be easier said than done. My ass is on the line, so I have to produce results.

I find it interesting that "Moses II" and I have something in common - our thoughts on the war are almost identical. I obviously object to his methods of showing his disagreement with our policies, but I do agree with his thinking about Iraq. We did a terrible job of understanding the relationships between the various tribal groups and religious factions in that country, and how much trouble there would be in trying to establish a democratic government there after Saddam was toppled. There were no weapons of mass destruction, and we have no business trying to be the world's policeman. American lives do not need to be shed just to get rid of some tinhorn dictator half-way around the world.

We might be better off without Saddam trying to stir up trouble, but getting rid of him is definitely not worth what it has cost us in lives, money, and goodwill with the rest of the world. But all we can do is call our reps in Congress, write letters, and show our concerns with our ballots. Terrorism is not the answer, and will not help to get our soldiers home any faster. As often as I would like to try and shake some sense into some of our members of Congress, burning their cars will not change their minds on how they vote. So as much as I like what Moses is standing up for, I can't let him do it the way he wants to do it. I'm going to catch him, and let our system work the way it is supposed to work.

I hate what our government has come to - ignoring the will of the people on this subject. And going into Iraq has not made us a safer country. I really fear for my wife and unborn child, knowing what I do about how the rest of the world feels about us, and what a lot of terrorists are trying to do to hurt our country. President Bush and his cronies have turned "America the Beautiful" into the bully of the playground - and I don't like what we have become, and how our actions may affect our own future. I'm sick about how low we have stooped, and how we are even growing our own terrorists because of the actions of a President that made C grades in school, and then surrounded himself with advisors that aren't any smarter than he is. But it is my job to catch this character Moses. And if I want my promotion, I have to do it. So I will go after him, and I will catch him. Even if I do sympathize with his motives, he is just another bad guy, and he is going down.

Chapter 3

Bill Peterson
FBI HQ
7:06 AM, Friday, July 21, 2006

We've heard from Moses again. The message was delivered this morning to the same media outlets and politicians he used the last time around. All the letters had a Washington postmark. No DNA, no fingerprints, nothing unusual about the print, ink, paper, or envelopes. To show the level of detail we go to when examining evidence, I can tell you that the ink from these letters came from an HP inkjet cartridge #56. When we find this guy, and check his printer, I bet it is a printer that can handle that particular cartridge.

We now have people checking the mail of everyone on this guy's mailing list as early as possible every day, trying to get as much notice as possible when he sends the next one (if we don't catch him in the interim!). All of the D.C. government mail is being irradiated before it is delivered, to kill whatever microbes someone tries to send to someone in power. The Post Office has been doing that since the anthrax attacks in 2001. The Postal Service (and a lot of other government agencies) also use "sniffers" of one sort or another to check for biological agents in the mail before it gets out of the mail room. Most agencies don't even let their mail be opened on site any more - it is done by a private contractor at a different location, so that we don't end up like we did in 2001 with the Longworth Building out of commission for months. Back then, that Congressional office building had to be fumigated to get rid of the anthrax spores that got loose when a staffer opened a letter containing "white powder." This new message will probably spread panic throughout the D.C. metropolitan area.

The latest warning letter has not yet been released to the public, but like Sally said this morning, making a bad pun, "Something like this will leak pretty quickly."

I wish I had stock in the local bottled water industry!

A WARNING TO THE COUNTRY'S POLITICAL LEADERSHIP

YOU DID NOT HEED MY FIRST WARNING.

SO, JUST AS GOD (THROUGH MOSES)

TURNED THE WATER IN EGYPT INTO BLOOD,

I HAVE MADE YOUR WATER UNFIT TO DRINK.

IF YOU HAVE BEEN DRINKING WATER FOR

THE PAST FEW DAYS, IT IS ALREADY TOO

LATE. THIS WILL NOT AFFECT EVERYONE, BUT IS AIMED AT THOSE THAT GOT AMERICA INTO THIS GODLESS WAR. YOU HAVE NOT BEEN POISONED, BUT YOU WILL BECOME DEATHLY ILL. SOME WILL DIE. PERHAPS WHILE YOU ARE ILL YOU SHOULD CONSIDER THE INTERPRETATIONS AND ADVICE THAT YOU GAVE THAT RESULTED IN AMERICA MEDDLING WHERE THE COUNTRY DOES NOT BELONG. FIND A WAY TO PULL THE AMERICAN TROOPS OUT OF IRAQ, AND START THE PROCESS BY THE END OF THIS CONGRESSIONAL TERM, OR YOU WILL PAY. AS MOSES SAID TO THE EGYPTIANS, "LET MY PEOPLE GO!" IF PROGRESS IS NOT SEEN RAPIDLY, MORE PLAGUES AND PESTILENCE

WILL RAIN DOWN UPON YOU, JUST AS DISCUSSED IN THE BOOK OF EXODUS. START THINGS MOVING TOWARD TOTAL WITHDRAWAL, OR YOUR DAYS ARE NUMBERED!

We have already gotten water samples from the various water districts from southern Virginia to Baltimore, and we have started testing for poisons, bacteria, and viruses. We haven't found anything yet - spectrometer results were negative for the things we think might be used as a biological/poison weapon. The lab people tell us that culture results will not be reliable until we reach the 48 hour mark. We already have stockpiles in the D.C. area of everything from ciprofloxacin, for anthrax, to antiviral drugs like interferon.

We have people checking security at every water processing plant in our area, and also checking the water sources for all of our drinking water. My thoughts are that we are too late, but that we might find some evidence to help us catch this turkey. We have better water supply security now than we used to, because poisoning our water supply has always been a viable threat. But it is still possible for someone to slip something through, as the warning letter suggests. We *think* the perp is referring to some part of the country's intelligence apparatus in this latest missive, most probably the CIA - but we're not sure. We are paying special attention to the McLean part of the metro area, but we are not limiting the scope of our investigation in any way until we get more data. The psych people say that the fact that he repeated part of his threat shows that he is determined enough to try and pull this off. Just what I needed to hear. Julie just called, and wants me to pick up some peanut butter on the way home. I guess the cravings are beginning. Mine and hers. She won't let me touch her, afraid of what it might lead to, and she wants to make sure she doesn't harm the baby. Some obstetricians claim you shouldn't have sex after the first trimester. I think Julie reads too much.

We also have a new member on my team. The Washington Post ran a scathing editorial on how the FBI couldn't catch a chicken in a chicken coop, even with all the modern tools we have on hand to help with evidence gathering. They went on and on about how we are trampling on the Bill of Rights, and still can't get the job done. So Director Mueller got on the phone with Donald Graham, the Chairman of the Post. After they got through yelling at each other, they made a deal. We are now assigned an "embedded" reporter, just like the ones assigned to travel with the army. We have been told to give this guy full access to everything we do, so that he can write (hopefully after we capture our terrorist) that we did it legally. His name is Bill Erickson, and he supposedly knows a little something about law enforcement. We will see. And I can't wait for the confusion that having two Bills on the team will cause.

Lester Home
McLean, VA
7:26 AM, Monday, July 24, 2006

"Mommy, my throat hurts. Can I stay home from camp today?"

"Cindy, did you check your blood sugar level?"

"Yes ma'am, it was fine. I took my shot already this morning. Now I just feel sweaty and my muscles hurt, and I feel like I'm going to throw up."

"OK, maybe we need to run you by the doctor's, just to make sure everything's fine."

Bill Peterson
FBI HQ
2:30 PM, Monday, July 24, 2006

Fairfax County in Virginia has a 120 page plan on how to deal with a Pandemic Influenza outbreak. Their plan was wrong in one respect, where they stated that the Pandemic would occur world-wide at the same time. It may develop into that, but right now it is pretty much limited to Fairfax and the surrounding counties. It looks like our guy somehow introduced some strain of the "bird flu" virus into Fairfax Water's Corbalis Treatment Plant, located just north of Great Falls on the Potomac. That plant services the northern part of Fairfax County, but it also sells some water to Loudon, Prince William County, and, more importantly to me, the city of Alexandria. Julie pretty much just drinks bottled water, but we still make coffee, brush our teeth, and wash off our dishes with what may be contaminated water. So we may have been exposed, too. We've been calling each other every couple of hours, just to make sure we are not symptomatic. The hospitals in the entire area are filling up with what looks like serious cases of Avian flu. No one has died yet, but there are a few people in critical condition - mostly those with weakened immune systems from already existing health conditions. Everybody infected so far either lives or works in an area served by Fairfax Water.

CIA headquarters in Langley has a set of deep water wells and a stand-alone purifying system, so that they don't need public water. However, to save money, they don't use that system unless it looks like there is a direct threat against the country! They have been using Fairfax Water's output for several years. The CIA Director, General Hayden, told Director Mueller that they were seeing a 30% absenteeism rate today, and expected it to get worse. Fairfax County has been declared a disaster area, and their Emergency Operations Center has been activated. We are assisting there, and trying to get information on visitors to the treatment plant during the past couple of weeks.

We have the Center for Disease Control people from Atlanta already in D.C., and more doctors and environmental health officials from all over the country are trying to get here just as fast as they can to help keep this from spreading. The army people from Ft. Deitrick are even prepared to cordon off that entire area, if an embargo is necessary to keep the disease in check. It looks like for sure that any chicken within 50 miles of D.C. will need to be destroyed, just to try and keep the outbreak from spreading into a true world-wide Pandemic. The scary part is that this part of the country is known as a flyway - wild birds migrate through here, going south in the fall, and north in the spring. If we can't get this under control quickly, there is a good chance that birds will spread this in a couple of months all the way to South America. Chicken is off my menu for a while, and I don't think I will be ordering duck at any Chinese restaurants, either.

I sat down with my team after lunch today, (along with Mr. Lawrence, again!) and we started brainstorming. We have lots of new questions, but not many answers. Charlie, the team's chemical and bioweapon expert, told us that one change was key.

He asked, "How did our guy, if it was the same guy, get the virus to remain viable in water?" He told us that "Up until now, people that caught this version of the flu had to be infected by being in close contact with an infected bird or pig. Does that mean that this group has access to a laboratory capable of modifying the old virus?"

Sally spoke up. "How did he get access to the water system? When did he introduce the virus?"

Andy said, "Charlie, why didn't the chlorine in the water kill the virus?"

Charlie told us all that while chlorine did a good job killing bacteria, it was not that great at stopping viruses. He said we had even more worries. "How infectious is the virus? Will it now spread to the rest of the area, the country, the world?"

My thoughts, that I kept to myself, were that we have a lot of people close to panic in Fairfax County, and some people in this building are beginning to look like they are close to the edge, too. My boss just left without saying another word. Maybe we got a little lucky on this one, but we don't even know enough to know what the incubation period is for this particular version of the flu virus. We won't know for sure that we are out of the woods for several more days. I know I'm rambling, but I'm tired. We all are. We were here until about 11 last night. As I stretched, just to get the blood circulating, Sally offered to give me a back rub. I thought seriously about taking her up on it. People don't think well under this much tension, and we have got to outthink these terrorists. I gave my team another pep talk.

"We have got to put a stop to this, and fast, before the entire country gets so paranoid that neighbors start shooting neighbors just for coming home after dark."

They didn't think it was funny, either.

INOVA Regional Trauma Center,
Fairfax County, VA
4:12 PM Monday July 24, 2006

"Mrs. Lester? I'm Doctor Edwards. We're doing everything we can for Cindy, but she is in a bad way. With her weakened immune system from the Juvenile Diabetes, the odds are not good."

"Can we see her?"

"That's not a good idea, especially since we do not know how easily this version of the flu spreads. Plus we have to be able to get to her at a moment's notice if her blood pressure drops any lower. She is in a coma from her high temperature, so she wouldn't know that you were there. I'll let you know if there is any change in her condition."

Bill Peterson
FBI HQ
3:22 PM Wednesday, July 26, 2006

Six people have died so far, including Cindy Lester, an eight-year-old girl from McLean. Whatever Robin Hood mantle people were putting on this guy after his attack on the Congressional parking lot is now gone. When you start killing innocent bystanders, especially children, you can't consider it to be funny or heroic. There are a few radicals in the Middle East claiming that this is God's revenge on the Great Satan, but they say the same thing every time a tornado touches down in Kansas, too. We don't have any proof that any Middle East organization is involved in this - but we don't have any proof that they aren't, either.

We still have some serious issues to handle. Every hospital in the area is full of very sick people, and more are expected to die over the next few days. Even two of our agents that live in Tyson's Corner are in the hospital, and the wife of one of our lab support people is in critical condition. The Health Department people have started destroying chicken flocks, and farmers are screaming - but we can't take chances that the chickens didn't drink some of the contaminated water, or pick up the virus from a stray bird in the area. The price of a carton of eggs in D.C. area supermarkets has doubled twice over the last three days, as eggs are being imported from as far away as Georgia.

The Post ran a front page picture today showing an aerial picture of the CIA parking area taken yesterday morning. There were only about 10 cars in the entire parking lot. The CIA Director had ordered all non-essential personnel to stay home the rest of the week, and it was pretty obvious from the picture that even some that were supposed to be at work didn't show. Whether they were sick, or just afraid of catching the disease has not been announced. Either way, our terrorist did a good job of shutting down that agency. They put out a press release about how "National security has not been compromised by people being out of the office," and "a lot of our employees are working from home using computers connected directly to the Agency." I hope that is true. If they did miss something important, I hope it doesn't come back to haunt us.

The good news is that the bug doesn't seem to be infectious from human to human without intimate contact, and the number of new cases fell off dramatically yesterday. We're hoping this was a short-term event, and it looks like we have avoided the pandemic we thought this might start. You never know when the flu bug will mutate into something really dangerous, and we will have another 1919 type epidemic with thousands (or millions) around the world dying from this disease. The CDC people are even starting to breathe again. They used a new system called Fluchip that tells the scientists within 12 hours what strain of flu they are working with. This seems to just be a substrain of the H2N2 Avian flu virus that sometimes mutates into something really dangerous - like the H3N2 version that caused the Hong Kong flu epidemic back in 1968 and 1969, that killed 750,000 people. However, it doesn't look like it has mutated in any of the cases they have seen so far in this area. We're not out of the woods yet, but there does seem to be a little pin point of light at the end of a very dark tunnel. And it turns out that Alexandria gets its water from a different Fairfax Water treatment plant, and not the one hit by our bad guy - so Julie and I dodged a bullet on this one.

Sally reported on what she had found out about Corbalis. The water treatment plant where we think all of this started gives tours 3 days per week, on Monday, Wednesday, and Friday. All people have to do to take the tour is show up on time, and sign a log. No ID required, no pictures taken. Some security! Whoever pulled this off seems to know where our weak points are, and is exploiting the cracks in the walls we thought were protecting us. The plant has two tour guides, and neither remembers anyone resembling our suspect on any of last week's tours. The closest we have been able to come is the name "Lisa Moshewitz" scribbled in their guest register from last Wednesday. "Moshe" is the Hebrew spelling of Moses. That may be a reach, but that's all we have at this point. Lisa did not list an address in the visitor's log. Larry Tidwell, the tour guide that gave the tour on Wednesday, told Sally that he doesn't remember much about "Lisa." He says she was tall, thin, blond, not particularly attractive, and that she hung with a family from Baltimore that was taking the tour. He assumed that she was with them, but had no proof to offer other than she was talking to them during the tour. He remembers her asking a question about water quality that made him think that she did know some chemistry or biology - something about what level of chloramines did the plant engineers think was necessary to keep Cryptosporidium down to a safe level? He said he gave her a copy of the Fairfax Water 2006 water quality report, and told her that the information she wanted was in the report.

We're trying to track down the Jones family that was on that same tour - the family that the tour guide said seemed to know Lisa Moshewitz. For their address, all they listed was "Baltimore, MD." Do you know how many families named Jones live in Baltimore? But we're good at this sort of thing. Sally bet me a Coke that we would have them by tomorrow. I told her Friday. I'm really hoping I have to buy her a soda. And as usual, the more we know, the more new questions we have. And the brass upstairs want answers yesterday. Moshewitz? Is that "I'm with Moses?" "I am Moses, but in disguise?" Or was

71

the culprit someone else that isn't even on our radar screen? Sally has also come up with another angle. I told you she doesn't miss many!

She asked me, "Why is this guy using this particular mailing list? Does he plan to attack every politician on the list?"

I passed her concerns up the line. My boss said that Director Mueller had already come up with the same idea.

He told me to tell her that "Just in case, we have doubled security at the State Department, Congress, and beefed up the personal security for Donald Rumsfeld, the Secretary of Defense. We figure the Pentagon can take care of itself, so we don't need to add protection there. The Secret Service does not want our help - they have been protecting the President and Vice-President for a long time, and they feel they know what they are doing."

If it is just one guy, you have to give him credit for pulling off two such ops within a couple of weeks. That took some pretty good planning in advance. Even some of our team members are convinced we are dealing with an entire cell, and not just one person - they think that the scouting required to pull off these two operations are too much for one person to have handled.

Bill Erickson, the reporter, asked a couple of good questions. "If it is just one guy, where did he learn to pull off such stunts? Has he been formally trained in one of the terrorist wannabe camps in Syria or Lebanon?"

Sally added, "Where did he get the flu germs that he let loose? Once we identify the exact bug, we can start narrowing down to the source."

We all have a lot more questions than we have answers at this point. My boss, Tom, keeps telling me that I am doing everything that can be done, and that he has full confidence in me. So far, I think that is close to the truth. Of course, a lot of pro football team owners announce that they have "full confidence" in their head coaches the week before they fire and replace the poor coach. That vote of support is almost considered the kiss of death in the sports arena. We need a break to catch this guy, group, whatever it is. And usually, somewhere down the road, everyone makes a mistake. I just hope I'm still here when we get that break.

Baltimore, MD
2:30 PM Friday, July 28, 2006

Sally and I drove to Baltimore together to interview the Jones family at their home. We could have let the local agents do it, but we felt this was too critical, and we wanted to drag every possible bit of information out of them, without making them feel like suspects. They were already sick about the fact that they had been walking around with a possible terrorist killer, and did not know it. The kids were 12, 9, and 7. The two oldest were boys, and the youngest a girl.

The family had gone to visit the plant because the oldest boy had an interest in chemistry, and they were trying to excite him about uses for that science. They obviously had never seen the "Moshewitz" girl before the tour. The dad told us that he had first noticed her as they were walking into the plant - she said something to the kids about how were they enjoying their summer as they were walking through the entrance. Jimmy, the 9-year-old, had the most interesting bit of info. He said that he had stopped to use the restroom during the tour, and as he was coming out and hurrying to join the rest of the group, he saw "Lisa" squatting down by one of the settling ponds, with her back to everyone else. He thought it was weird, but didn't say anything to anyone about it at the time.

Phyllis, Mrs. Jones, said, "You know, the girl seemed a little odd to me. I can't put my finger on it, but there was something a little strange about her. For one thing, she didn't seem to flirt with either of my boys, my husband, or the guy leading the tour. And you know that for a young American female, flirting is a full-time sport."

Sally laughed and agreed. Sally asked them if they thought it could have been a guy in disguise, and both Mr. and Mrs. Jones said that it was possible. They said that they were paying pretty close attention to their three kids during the tour, trying to keep them out of trouble, and did not take the time to closely examine the "girl" trying to tag along with them. They told us about the picture "Lisa" had taken of all of them, and we told them we had to confiscate their camera, and take it in for checks for fingerprints and DNA. We took cheek swab samples from each member of the family, so that any other DNA on the camera would show up as possibly our suspect's. I promised they would get the camera back in pristine condition. We set up an appointment with one of our sketch artists, so that they could give us a drawing of our suspect. On the way back to the car Sally tried to convince me that "Lisa" was our guy from the fire at National. She said everything still pointed to just one person, and we had to find him before he pulled another stunt like the first two - or worse.

Sally seemed a little quiet on the ride back, considering the progress we had made questioning the Jones family, so I asked her if anything was wrong. She blushed a little, which I found charming, and she wouldn't look at me.

She said, "I don't want to dump my personal problems on you - you're my boss!"

"If you are thinking about something other than the case, then maybe you do need to talk about your personal problems. Advice is cheap."

She kept looking out the window to her right. She said, "Well, you know I've started dating a new guy. His name is Wally Brookstone, and he's a Texan, just like you. But that's about all you have in common. He's a Texas A&M grad that still thinks the Aggie Corps of Cadets could walk on water if they wanted to. He just started working for the Army Corps of Engineers, and he is terribly gung ho about all that spit and polish BS. My problem is that he is not only dumber than a box of rocks, but that he isn't that romantic, either." She took a big breath, and continued, "He does have one redeeming feature. He is the greatest kisser I've ever dated, but that's all he will do. He gets me hot, and then gets up and says, 'goodnight.' I'm beginning to think he may be gay."

"He wouldn't be dating you if he was gay. He's probably just inexperienced, and this will give you a chance to train him right. But I'm prejudiced. You have to remember that I'm a graduate of the University of Texas, and we don't think much of people that went to Texas A&M. In Austin, we think that an Aggie's idea of a hot date is a sheep in summer pasture."

She laughed a little at that, but kept looking out the side window of the car. Her exasperated response was, "Well, he seems to be happy with how things are going, and I don't see things changing, no matter how hard I try."

"Well, then the next best thing is to dump him and find someone else."

"Do you know the ratio of single women to men in this town?" was her terse reply.

At that I shut up, deciding that I was out of my league in this conversation. Besides, there were dangerous connotations here that I really didn't want to even consider. Thinking about Sally not having sex when I was pretty frustrated, too,

76

was not doing much to help me concentrate on driving in heavy traffic during rush hour on the Interstate. We rode the rest of the way back in silence. Just as we pulled back into the Bureau parking garage, she tried to apologize to me for dumping her personal situation on me.

"No problem," I said. "I did ask you what was wrong. I appreciate you feeling that you could trust me."

She smiled at me for the first time all afternoon. "Thanks, Bill," and a squeeze of my hand.

I felt like I was back in high school, taking a first date to her front door.

Robert Smithson
Journal Entry
July 28, 2006

I've been back in the lab in North Carolina for over a week now, catching up from my last few days of "vacation" in the Washington area. Of course, no one knows that I went to D.C. at any time this summer. I don't want any connections made between me and the events that took place in the Capital, or that will take place there in the next few months. I am trying to reduce the chances that I might run into someone that knows me when I'm in the D.C. area - someone from the military that knew me when I was growing up on military bases, someone that might know me from my undergraduate days at the University of

Florida, or one of my professors or classmates here at UNC. I'll stay away from the National Science Foundation, Fort Belvoir, and avoid the entire area if possible during seminars and events which would bring people in my field to Washington.

I still have to show some progress on my "normal" lab projects, and I still have to make lab reports every couple of weeks to my PI - the professor (Principal Investigator) that runs this lab. I can fool him for a while with no progress, but eventually I will have to produce results, or move on. I'm on a National Institute of Health grant that pays my personal and science equipment expenses while I'm doing research in this lab, so in a way when I am off doing my own thing I am taking their money under false pretenses. I don't think they would appreciate knowing that they are helping to fund my attacks on the government!

The fun part of this particular "plague" was redesigning the virus to be able to survive in water for up to 72 hours. I enjoy solving a good challenge. I actually got the idea from an old Tom Clancy novel, where he had some of the bad guys working with Ebola, another virus that doesn't survive long in the open. Tom had his characters add cancer DNA to the genes in the virus to strengthen the virus, so that it could live long enough in the open air to be inhaled after being sprayed into the air from a water vapor/cooler. Adding cancer DNA to Ebola genes would not really work, but there are a lot of viruses that do survive surprisingly well in water, like polio. It was not difficult for someone that has been working with viruses for as long as I have to recombine some of the DNA from the polio virus into the flu virus capsid.

I started with the basic H2N2 virus that caused the global flu outbreak back in 1957 and 1958. Samples of that virus were distributed in proficiency test kits world-wide back in 2005 (allegedly by mistake) by the College of American Pathologists. After they realized that this was a pretty big blunder, they put out a press release a few days later about how "99% of the test kits had been tracked down and destroyed." That was bull. I'll bet that half the labs that received the H2N2 strain in the test kits sent out by CAP kept a sample, just in case they needed it to play with during a pandemic sometime in the future. Some of my fellow graduate students at UNC kept a sample, and I had no problem "borrowing" some of that sample from their lab.

I hope my new virus does not mutate into something that does more damage than I want it to do. My tests seem to show that the current version can survive a few days in water (as long as the water is not boiled), and it shouldn't (I hope!) spread from person to person without close contact. I'm not trying to start a pandemic. All I wanted to do at this point is punish the people at the CIA that got us into this war. Their stupidity is matched only by the people that didn't plan for post-war complications, but that is something that I will deal with in the future. The CIA was my target, and I pretty well succeeded in shutting them down for a few days. Every time someone at the CIA takes a drink of water in the future, I want them to remember the punishment that was dished out because of their errors in judgment. Hopefully that will make them be a little more careful with their extrapolations the next time they have to make a projection on threat capabilities.

We have pretty well perfected a gene splicing system here in our lab. We use enzymes to cut the DNA strands at various points on each strand, and then mix the strands from two different genes (like ones from Polio and Avian Flu viruses). All you have to do at that point is reintroduce the "new" strands back into the virus, and see which ones work best. That is a much easier process than trying to get specific strands tied together. We can do that too, but it is still difficult to know which strands control what. So if we need a strand that makes the gene (and the virus) survive better in water, we mix the genes, put them back together, put them in water and see which ones survive. That method is much faster than the trial and error efforts of the past, and gets us to the goal much more efficiently.

The hardest part of my campaign so far was shaving my legs! I couldn't show up at the water treatment plant in shorts with hairy legs, pretending to be a girl. My disguise was pretty good. I paid top dollar for the wig in Charlotte, and spent hours practicing putting on makeup and doing my nails before I ever got to D.C. I even hid the female disguise stuff from the motel room cleaning ladies - I didn't want them wondering why a guy had a bag full of women's makeup in his bathroom, and women's clothing in the closet. These days cross-dressing is not as rare as it used to be, but I didn't want to be gossiped about by the motel staff.

After preparing my disguise, I snuck out the back door of the motel so that I wouldn't have to go by the front desk. I pulled into the treatment plant's parking lot 10 minutes before the tour was scheduled to start, and waited until a minivan pulled in down the row from me. I walked in with that family, already talking to their kids like I was a part of their group. Family groups look much less suspicious compared to loners. While I didn't look like a wild-eyed Arab toting an Uzi, I didn't want to give the treatment plant people any reason to want to pay me special attention. It might have been very awkward if they had asked to search my oversized purse, and found the quart bottle of "water" that I was carrying!

I did get carried away momentarily when I was asked to sign in - I couldn't resist the Moshewitz moniker. The "Lisa" I used as a first name was the first name that popped into my mind. I wonder if I will ever forget her, or if there is still some slim chance that I could get her to run off with me when this is over? Using either of those names was probably a mistake, but I do like tweaking the FBI's nose a lot. I know they are chomping at the bit to find me, and I don't want to make it any easier for them. Even the questions I asked might have drawn attention that I don't really need. I'll try and avoid such egocentric acts in the future. I was afraid someone would take my picture while I was there, but I avoided that by offering to take a picture of the entire Jones family for them, giving them a souvenir of their tour. I made sure I wiped my prints off of their camera before I gave it back to them.

And speaking of the FBI, I now know the name of the guy that is leading the group after me. The Washington Post did an article on Bill Peterson, talking about his success in the past in catching bad guys all around the country. I'm tempted to send him a note along the lines of "I'm the Gingerbread Man and you can't catch me!" But I don't want to give him any extra incentive to help motivate him, or any extra clues as to my whereabouts. He sounds competent, but he probably would be good at what he does, or else he wouldn't be in charge of the team chasing me. I've taken precautions, in case the Fibbies get too close, but I hope I don't have to use them for a while.

The sad part of this operation was the picture of Cindy Lester on the front page of the Raleigh News & Observer today. I do feel sorry for her family. No parent should have to bury their child. But then, no child should have to bury a parent that hasn't had a chance to live a long and full life - something that military families all over the country are being forced to do all too often when their loved ones are shipped home in a box from Iraq. I still have a conscience, and I can't just be flippant about the deaths in Virginia, and say something like you have to break a few eggs to make an omelet. It bothers me that I have killed some innocent people. But I can overcome that when I think about my long term goal. I was trained growing up to be goal oriented, and to let nothing get in the way of obtaining a goal once it is set.

I did enjoy the picture in the paper of the empty parking lots at Langley. I hope people in power are beginning to realize that there may be consequences for the decisions they make and the advice they give. I read the nasty things people are saying about me, but they still do not understand that my motives are pure, even if the acts that I perform make for occasional unintended consequences. My next few operations should be more selective, but even in these some people may suffer that were not part of the decision to go to war. If I win in the end, my conscience will be clear.

One thing that I hated about this part of the campaign is that it will make Donald Rumsfeld that much richer. He is the largest stockholder in Gilead Sciences, the company that makes Tamiflu - one of the antivirus medications that more companies (and the government) will stock up on just in case this attack gets repeated somewhere else. There are now some concerns about that drug, due to some potential side effects identified in Japan. I hope the drug has problems, and is pulled off the market. I hate to see any of my potential targets profiting in any way from the war, or even a protest of that war. And I don't even want to get into discussing the oil buddies of President Bush, or who all owns stock in Halliburton. The tax burden from this war will come due sooner or later, and inflation will go way back up because of the cost of bonds when the government tries to borrow more money to pay for the shortfall in our country's budget. Of course, that will get blamed on the next administration - it always works that way. Perhaps we can save a few billion if I can get us out of Iraq a year or two sooner than currently planned. Saving your tax dollars - that's me!

The dates are already set for the next few events on my calendar. It is always very helpful for public relations people to publish itineraries far in advance - it makes planning for events much more simple when you know exactly where your next target will be at a certain time on a certain date. I started this campaign with a JASON timeline - two attacks in July, using August for final preparations, one plague in September, and two in October. The "N" in JASON is for November, and I hope the last two plagues I have scheduled for that month are not necessary. Perhaps by that time Congress will have acted, or else the President will have declared the war won, and started to bring our people back to the United States. That's fine with me if that strategy is what he needs to use to save face. I don't care how he does it, but we need to start withdrawing forces. I'm not sure Bush is smart enough to see that all he has to do is announce a victory, and leave. Or he may be too stubborn to even want to try that bit of flim/flam. We will see. I will do what it takes, all the way through the fall if necessary. Some of these will be riskier to me than others, but I will take what precautions I can to stay anonymous. I will use the time remaining to finish preparing my bag of tricks. Halloween is not that far away, and I have curses to brew.

Chapter 4

Bill Peterson
Georgetown University Medical Center
5:45 AM September 7, 2006

Now it is personal. If I can get to this guy before anyone else, he will not live to make it in front of a jury. We lost the baby. Julie is in the hospital here, along with Condoleezza Rice, the Secretary of State. Both are listed as being in "serious" condition. A couple of hours ago they were both critical. Both Jean-David Levitte, the French Ambassador to the United States, and Nicholas Burns, the U.S. Under Secretary for Political Affairs, died about an hour ago. 22 others, mostly American State Department employees or French Embassy staffers, are in hospitals here in D.C. All are suffering from various levels of Ricin poisoning, ingested with their dinner last night, hosted by the State Department. Somehow this modern day Moses got to the food, either at the dinner, or more probably at the caterer's.

I've been at the hospital since about 10 PM with Julie. People started getting sick within about 30 minutes of starting dinner. At first, everyone thought it was probably just food poisoning - not poisoned food. As people started to get sicker, ambulances were called, and emergency rooms in this area filled up again. Within about an hour they had the poison identified.

Blood in the stool, a sign of gastric bleeding, was a hint for a sharp doctor that probably saved my wife's life, along with some of the others. There is no antidote for Ricin poisoning. If you ingest enough of it, you die. However, some labs have started working with goats as test subjects, developing antibodies that seem to help reduce the severity of the results when the poison enters the body. They used those experimental drugs on Julie and Condi Rice, and that probably saved both of them. But either the Ricin, or the side effects from the antidote, killed our baby. Doctor Albert Bellamy, the guy that saved my wife, says that she will be able to have other children, and that I should consider us lucky because she will pull through. He told me that he had just finished a seminar on poisons and infectious diseases, because he was working in D.C. and felt that he needed to be prepared to handle WMDs. That seminar raised his level of consciousness about the stuff, so when he spotted the symptoms he was able to make the correct diagnoses quickly. He told me that ingesting the poison is actually less dangerous than inhaling the stuff, or the even worst possibility of getting it injected directly into the bloodstream. Ricin is what killed Georgi Markov, a Bulgarian dissident living in London, back in 1978. The Russians got to him with a poisoned umbrella tip. That case is studied by every class coming through the FBI Academy. I know what Ricin can do, and I'm glad it looks like Julie will pull through. But I'm still mad as hell.

Apparently the people still living this morning did not get a full dose like the French Ambassador and Under Secretary absorbed, and that helped them survive, too. The doctor says that the poison oxidizes quickly, and becomes less dangerous after being exposed to air or water for just a short time. The lab here at the hospital and the one at Headquarters are both trying to analyze the frog legs to determine how much Ricin was in each leg. Did I mention the frog legs were poisoned? Karen Hughes, the former Bush associate and now State Department Under-Secretary for Public Diplomacy and Public Affairs, told my team that she hated frog legs, and asked for chicken as a replacement. Karen said that Secretary Rice always just played with her food at these dinners, preferring to use the time to talk business, but that Ambassador Levitte was putting down "les cuisses de grenouilles" like they were hot wings at Hooters. No one was paying any attention to my wife - just another staffer at the dinner - but it looks like she ate enough to nearly kill her. She was eating for two, and however much she ate it was too much for the baby.

September 6th is Lafayette's birthday, and it is traditional that the United States honors France on that date, to thank them for sending the Marquis to help save our bacon during the Revolutionary War. The French still feel that we would have never obtained our freedom from the British without their help. Of course, they also think that Charles de Gaulle won World War II, and we were just along for the ride. The dinner is on the State Department's calendar and website well in advance, so I'm sure this is Moses acting up again. The dinner, held in the Jefferson Building at the Library of Congress, was catered by Occasions Catering. They are well known as gourmet caterers, and they handle a good bit of the government's dinners around town. I'm sure we will find that Moses was somehow involved with the food preparation or delivery.

We haven't received the usual letter yet, but I bet it is in the mail, and probably scheduled for delivery later this morning. Agents have already gone to the Post Office (including some Postal Inspectors to make us going through the mail seem at least a little legal) to look through mail already sorted for delivery to the media outlets that usually get Moses' threats. I'm still at the hospital, waiting for Julie to wake.

Even though we are personally involved, so far they haven't pulled me off the case. Usually when there is a personal involvement the agent will get shifted to other duties. I've already pleaded with Tom to go to bat for me - I want to stay after this guy. Something in my favor is that I'm no longer in charge. We are now an inter-agency task force, with representatives on board from every law enforcement and 3-letter spook group that the President and his staff could come up with. We're now led by Mark Sullivan, the head of the Secret Service - and that shows the importance the President has suddenly put on this case. My team is now just a subgroup of the task force, taking orders from Mr. Sullivan. Tom Lawrence is one of Mr. Sullivan's vice-chairs on the task force, so I still report through him. We have a briefing scheduled at 8 AM this morning to bring everyone else up to speed on what we know, what we suspect, and what we need to find out before this guy kills again.

Sally has been tasked with organizing the interviewing of the catering people. We want to find out if there was someone new in their group, someone hired from a temp agency, or someone new back at the caterer's kitchen. This guy had to show himself to pull this one off, and we should be able to get a good description from someone on the caterer's staff. He is obviously now on our top ten wanted list, and there are rewards posted for his apprehension. Every time this guy pulls something, we gain more information about him - and sooner or later it will pay off and we will find him. I hope he resists arrest.

Homeland Security Headquarters
8:35 AM Thursday, September 7, 2006

We are across from the White House on E Street, in a big stuffy meeting room at Homeland Security, with each departmental team lecturing on what has happened, what we know, and suggestions on how to move forward from this point. We have a pretty good composite drawing from the people working for Occasions Catering. The "new guy" had apparently been there for around a week, helping out in the kitchen, and working a couple of dinners as a server prior to this one. He was described as having dark hair, a moustache, and an earring. He is blue-eyed, and the size fits the earlier descriptions and pictures we have of him from the airport fire and the water plant. He obviously gave the caterer a false name, address, and social security number, but we will follow up on that information just in case. He didn't expect to be there long enough for a paycheck to be cut. We also have his notice about this hit - a day too late to do us any good.

A WARNING TO THE COUNTRY'S POLITICAL LEADERSHIP

YOU DID NOT HEED MY FIRST WARNING, OR MY SECOND. SO, JUST AS GOD (THROUGH MOSES) SENT A PLAGUE OF FROGS INTO EGYPT, I HAVE USED FROGS TO REMIND THOSE THAT HELP DEVELOP THE AMERICAN FOREIGN POLICY THAT YOU NEED TO

CHANGE YOUR WAYS. THOSE OF YOU THAT ADVISE THE PRESIDENT ON THESE ISSUES SHOULD TAKE HEED, AND INSURE THAT THE PROCESS TO BRING HOME THE COALITION TROOPS BEGINS QUICKLY. THIS TIME IT IS POISON. THOSE THAT EAT THE FROGS WILL BECOME DEATHLY ILL. SOME WILL DIE. PERHAPS WHILE YOU ARE ILL YOU SHOULD CONSIDER THE INTERPRETATIONS AND ADVICE THAT YOU GAVE, AND CONTINUE TO GIVE, THAT RESULTS IN AMERICA MEDDLING WHERE THE COUNTRY DOES NOT BELONG. FIND A WAY TO PULL THE AMERICAN TROOPS OUT OF IRAQ, AND START THE PROCESS BEFORE THE END OF THIS CONGRESSIONAL TERM, OR YOU WILL

92

PAY. AS MOSES SAID TO THE EGYPTIANS, "LET MY PEOPLE GO!" IT TOOK THE PHARAOH TEN PLAGUES BEFORE HE LEARNED. HOW LONG WILL IT TAKE YOU? IS THREE ENOUGH, OR DO I HAVE TO STRIKE AGAIN, AND AGAIN, AND AGAIN? WILL IT TAKE SEVEN TIMES SEVEN? IF PROGRESS IS NOT SEEN RAPIDLY, MORE PLAGUES AND PESTILENCE WILL RAIN DOWN UPON YOU, JUST AS DISCUSSED IN THE BOOK OF EXODUS. START THINGS MOVING TOWARD TOTAL WITHDRAWAL, OR YOUR DAYS ARE NUMBERED!

A guy from the DIA brought up the point that our unsub had now used two fairly sophisticated elements in his attacks - Ricin and the Avian flu virus. The point he was making was that our guy had to have a pretty good lab somewhere to work on these WMDs, and now that we have a drawing, we should start hitting labs to see if anyone recognizes the bastard. Director Mueller told the group that he had over a thousand agents in the field available to help. He said that as soon as the picture could be emailed to every office, our people would start questioning private lab directors and educational institutions. We will also be querying lab supply places, to see if anything has been ordered to help someone set up their own lab. It might work - we could get lucky.

One of the behaviorists came next, and he started explaining that our guy seemed to be getting more frustrated, and therefore more dangerous - but also more likely to do something rash, so that there are better possibilities that we might find some solid evidence to help catch him. Mark mentioned that this guy keeps referring to the Old Testament plagues, and perhaps we ought to study those plagues in Exodus, to get some clues as to what he might be planning for the future.

A secretary came in, whispered something to one of the Secret Service guys in the back, and he pointed at me. She came over with a message from the hospital - Julie had regained consciousness, and was asking for me. I whispered to Sally that she was now in charge of our team, and to let me know if I missed anything important. I headed back to Georgetown and the Medical Center. I had told the doctors that I should be the one to tell her about the baby. Not a chore I'm looking forward to. God, I want to catch this guy and strangle him for what he has done to my family! I know I will not be able to console Julie. She wanted this baby so badly. Why can't we find one lousy terrorist? Is there some sort of support group helping him? I would love to be able to tell her that this was over, and we had him. But I can't, and I can't even say that we are making good progress towards catching him. As frustrated as I am, people need to stay out of my way. If some guy cuts me off with his car, I'm liable to shoot him.

Georgetown University Medical Center
9:40 AM Thursday, September 7, 2006

The first thing Julie said when I walked in the door was, "Bill, I lost the baby. They won't tell me anything, but I can tell. What's going on?"

I told her about the Ricin in the frog legs, the deaths, and how she had been treated with an experimental antidote. I told her that I had called her mom down in Waco, and that Margaret was flying to D.C. to be with her daughter. I tried to tell her how sorry I was. By this time we were both crying.

All Julie could do was keep moaning, "Why, God? Why me?"

I didn't have an answer for her, and God wasn't talking. I vowed to myself that I would get this guy, if I had to look for him the rest of my life. Doctor Bellamy came in, and started repeating the lines he had given me about how lucky Julie was, how she still had opportunities for children in the future, blah, blah, blah. At that point we didn't feel too lucky at all. All I could do at that point was sit there and hold her hand.

Julie got mad, wanting to take her frustrations out on someone, and I was the only one available. "Why weren't you here when I woke up? Are your damn career goals more important to you than me, your wife? What difference would it have made if you skipped one more silly meeting, when all you are doing anyway is spinning your wheels? Are you married to that job of yours, or do I really count for something in your life? Where were you when I needed you the most?"

What could I say? I was feeling guilty for failing to catch this turkey, failing to protect people in the Washington area, and especially for failing to protect my wife. Her accusations had a ring of truth to them that I couldn't refute. I sat there and took her abuse. I deserved it. In two months we had gone from the top of the world to a hell that I wouldn't wish on anyone.

Robert Smithson
Journal Entry
September 7, 2006

I've been busy since dropping the flu virus into the Fairfax County water supply. There have been too many people that have seen my face, including some good eye witnesses from the caterer's shop this past week. I knew that the more I showed myself, the greater the odds that a description good enough to identify me would go out, and then my days at this lab would be numbered. I did use a little bit of disguise at the caterers - I added an earring (clip on), grew a moustache, and dyed my hair dark. That will not slow the FBI down too much, but every little bit of disinformation will help.

I've spent the time since my attack on the CIA perfecting the remaining items I needed for the rest of my "plagues." I've got everything hidden in places away from the lab, scattered throughout the country. I've spent months perfecting a second identity, doing it the way the old Ian Fleming 007 books said to do it - find the birth date of a baby that died as an infant, request a copy of the birth certificate, and then use that to get further ID. I've got credit cards, bank accounts, a driver's license, and even a passport in the name James Smith. James is my middle name, and Smith is close enough to Smithson that I can remember it when I start to sign for rental cars or on hotel registers. It takes time to build up an identity, and that is another reason that I've had to wait months before striking back.

It also helps having plenty of money for travel expenses. My dad's life insurance policy left me enough cash that I can afford this campaign. If I survive this, I may immigrate to Australia or New Zealand - if the United States does not change its policies in the Middle East and bring our troops home, I don't think I will want to live here anymore. Not to mention that the FBI will always be looking for me! Because of my worries about being caught, I have decided to take my act on the road.

As of today, Robert Smithson no longer exists. If and when the FBI finally locates Smithson, and I'm sure they will eventually, it will be a dead end. I will leave for the lab on my bike from my apartment this morning just like I always do, but I will never set foot in that lab again. When the FBI comes looking, I will be someone else, and somewhere else. I will have very little personal exposure on these next attacks, so the odds of the FBI finding me before I finish all seven plagues is minimal. They are good, but I'm smart, and well trained. I'm pretty sure I can avoid capture long enough to complete my mission, and that is my prayer every night. Revenge is a dish best served cold. I am past the immediate heat of my loss. Cold logic will help me remain mistake free, and successful at what I do. Patience is a key, and that is why I took months to make sure I could do this right. I even spent hours relearning a skill I had honed as a kid - how to fly a radio controlled model airplane. If airplanes were good enough bombs on 9/11, a model airplane will be good enough for my purposes. I hope I can teach my kids how to fly model planes one day, and that I will not need to use my plane as a weapon in November. But like the Boy Scouts taught me, it is better to be prepared!

The Ricin was one of the easiest things to manufacture, but it took time. Finding enough Castor beans was easy. It is amazing how many of those plants are used as decorative foliage in North Carolina. Harvesting the beans was only the first step. Purifying the Ricin meant running the beans through an aqueous extraction process at a slightly acidic pH (that means you wash the beans). I don't want copycats, so the actual formula I will leave to the experts. If some kid ends up reading this journal, I don't want him trying this at home! I took the resulting leachate, filtered it, precipitated it back into a powder using sodium sulfate, and then washed the residue Ricin with a stronger solution of sodium sulfate to help clean it. After I "cooked" enough of these beans, always using a vent hood to make sure I wasn't breathing any stray Ricin molecules, I vacuum sealed the powder to keep it from oxidizing as long as possible. Ricin is soluble in water - so when I was ready to use it, all I had to do was drop a packet into a little water, which dissolved my packaging. I sucked that mix up into a syringe, and was ready to start injecting the poison into the frog legs.

I've also finished preparations on my October surprises - two more bugs that will put a further scare into the entire country. I've got everything stored in rental storage units in various places around the country, near where I plan to use them. I don't want to make it too easy for the FBI, so I haven't left any traces of any of my materials in my lab, or in my apartment. For November, I have a couple of big bangs planned, and the resources are in place at those locations if I need them. As I said earlier, I would prefer not to use those - maybe by that time the people in power will start to see the light. Otherwise, I'll have to start turning off the lights.

I've seen a couple of editorials from around the country starting to talk about how we need to bring our troops home, anyway - with or without the threats I keep making. It took a groundswell from the public to show the Johnson and Nixon administrations that the war in Vietnam was widely unpopular. I'm hoping that my actions help to precipitate the same type of feelings in Americans today. If people keep hearing about an illegal war, and if I can keep the body count from Iraq on the front pages, then people will start to wonder why we are there. We need to let Iraq solve its own problems. We've proven over and over that we cannot be the policeman for the entire world - all that does is make us more enemies, as we are perceived as a bully, trying to force our way of life on everyone else. President Bush keeps saying that our presence there is necessary for Iraq's survival. But is our presence there necessary for *our* survival? I think not, and in time, I feel that enough will agree with me to help get our people out of there. If the contractors want to stay in Iraq and help rebuild, let them -

but we don't have to be there just to protect Donnie Rumsfeld's buddies. George Bush called me a "psychopath" in a press conference today, as a response to a reporter's question on what the President thought about me and my attacks. He is probably right. I am a psychopath. I'll do whatever it takes to accomplish my goals, and if a few innocent people have to die along the way to get to the greater goal - getting our troops out of Iraq - so be it.

Getting the job at Occasions Caterers was a piece of cake. One of my roommates from my undergrad days down at the University of Florida was a waiter and helped in the kitchen at a high class restaurant in Gainesville called the Melting Pot. I used his name, and the restaurant as a reference, to get hired in Washington. I don't think they even bothered to check the reference. They might now! I knew about the State Department dinner well in advance (thank you public relations people and the Internet), and finding out that the caterer had ordered frog legs for the dinner was a nice coincidence. In this country frog legs are mostly a Cajun delicacy, and they can be ordered from Louisiana wholesalers year-round. Someone, either some protocol person at the State Department, or someone at the caterers, made the decision to serve them to the French at the banquet. What a great idea, and it worked out wonderfully for me. I was prepared to "doctor" the normal entrees of chicken or steak for the dinner, but the use of frog legs caused me to have to redo my threat letter at the last minute, to mention the plague of frogs in Egypt. I had to get new letters printed in D.C., and do so without leaving any traceable evidence on the letters or envelopes. I found an all-night copy place, and managed to wear some thin gloves while stuffing the envelopes. Self-sticking stamps help to keep from leaving DNA on the back of the stamps, because there is no need to lick. I hate changing plans at the last minute, but I couldn't resist using the reference to the original frog plague described in Exodus.

I volunteered to help prepare the dinner, telling my boss I could use the overtime. Coming in early that afternoon, I made sure that I was assigned to inject each frog leg with tenderizer. I also made sure that the tenderization process included my Ricin dissolved in water. I knew that the water, and then cooking the legs, would weaken the effects of the poison because of the oxidation problem, so I made sure that there was plenty of poison in each leg. To kill 50% of the people at the dinner, what is known as LD50 (for lethal dose) I had to make sure that they got at least 30 mcg/kg. That is the equivalent of 2 heavily poisoned frog legs, or 3 legs with a weakened dose.

When I first set up this attack I really wanted to kill Condoleezza Rice, but then I changed my mind and decided to just try and get her attention. So I wasn't that worried about the reduced dose that each frog leg would contain after being cooked. Secretary Rice was one of the main proponents of us going to war in Iraq, and she needed to be punished severely for her actions before the war. In her old job as National Security Adviser she was one of the people telling President Bush that we had to stop Saddam before he developed weapons of mass destruction, and that if we did not bring him down, sooner or later he would use those weapons. How much she was prejudiced by the faulty information coming out of the CIA I don't know. But I do know that Bush trusts her advice over almost everyone else's. That is one reason he nominated her to be Secretary of State after Colin Powell left the office. If she was out of the picture, then maybe he might start listening to other points of view.

One thing she has going for her is that she and Don Rumsfeld do not get along. There have been reports that the President had to step in, and tell Rumsfeld that he had to return her calls. Maybe, privately, she is starting to see how stupid it is that we are wasting our resources in Iraq. She still has to publicly support the President's position, but maybe she is a convert! If so, I'm now glad she survived. As for Rumsfeld, I will deal with him later.

I know the French were outraged that they were involved in this incident, but they deserved it, too. They flaunted the embargoes during Saddam's regime, allowing Iraq to buy "agricultural" machinery that could be used to make bioweapons, just to make a few Euros. Hussein would not have been able to act like he was preparing WMDs without the help of the French. I don't feel sorry for their ambassador or the embassy staff at all.

The next two months will have a huge impact on the current Washington regime. Either they need to get their act together on the Iraqi policy, or I will help things change through attrition. In each of my earlier warnings, I used the end of this Congressional term as a target date. That date is coming up in the first week of October - Congress is adjourning early, so that people that need to can go home and campaign for reelection. If Congress does not act to help get our guys and gals back, I will have to take action against that body again. They still have a month to act. If not, they will look back at the car fires as small potatoes.

I know the election in November may change the balance of power in both houses, but I can't take that chance. I blame the Republicans for the mess we are in. I know a lot of Democrats originally supported the war, based on the bad advice they were getting at the time, but now it is the Republicans that are keeping our people over there. I am going to go ahead and issue one more warning, and hopefully the message will be strong enough to get a positive reaction in D.C. If nothing happens before Congress adjourns *sine die*, then some will need to die.

Bill Peterson
FBI Office, Raleigh, NC
08:00 AM Tuesday September 19, 2006

For a few hours my teammates and I were treated like heroes here at the Bureau. Through dogged detective work, we identified a good "subject of interest," a guy named Robert Smithson, Jr. We were getting all sorts of praise, the public relations people were prepared to put out news releases about how we caught the guy, and the entire office was in a much better mood. Tom Lawrence was of course taking full credit for finding the guy, but his bosses knew who had really put in the work.

Unfortunately, it looks like he had already skipped. We thought we had the guy, but it looks like we're still somewhere behind him. We at least now know who he is, but suddenly we don't look quite as good to our bosses. We were following up with all the university labs in the country, using the picture developed from the eyewitness accounts from the caterers. We used one of our computer programs to take that picture and morph it into a blond guy with and without facial hair, and as a woman with various hair colors. We weren't sure what disguises this guy was using, so we tried to cover every possibility. All of those possible pictures went to every FBI office in the country. An agent from Raleigh was interviewing at the University of North Carolina when a sharp secretary told him that she thought our blond picture looked like one of their doctoral candidates, studying biochemistry.

We have his lab and his apartment staked out, waiting for him to show. He apparently lives alone in an apartment complex called Sterling Bluffs in Carrboro, a bedroom community adjoining Chapel Hill and the University. We moved people in today to a vacant apartment across from his, and we have people staked out on the lab, but we haven't seen him so far at either location. We had his Principal Investigator, the guy that runs his particular lab on campus, called to the Dean's Office. Doctor Bowman, the PI, told us that Mr. Smithson had not been seen around the lab in the last week. He said that Smithson had called the previous week, claiming that he was depressed over his dad's death, and had asked for a leave of absence from the lab. I'm afraid he has skipped, worrying that we were on his trail after the Ricin attack. We have tracers out on his credit cards, ATM card, and we have asked a federal judge for phone taps on his family's phones, in case he tries to contact them. We are watching the Ft. Bragg area, obviously the D.C. area, and even Gainesville, FL, where our suspect did his undergraduate work.

We have his records from the University, and they show he is smart. His transcript also shows that he has had classes in chemistry and the biological sciences, all the way up to gene therapy research in his lab. His professor agrees that he had the skill set to have pulled off the

Ricin and the flu virus attacks. We haven't found any traces of the stuff he has used in the lab, but all that says is that he cleans up well. We are still looking for other possible things he might use in future attacks. We also have information on his possible motivation. Dr. Bowman told us about Smithson's dad being killed in Iraq earlier this year.

His car is still sitting in the apartment complex parking lot, so he has to be using some other form of transportation. His neighbors tell us he had a bike, but he obviously couldn't get very far on that. We are reviewing film at all the rental car agencies in the area, checking tapes of the bus stations, and even talking to car dealerships. He may have skipped, but we are right on his tail. When we get someone on the run, it usually doesn't take long. He will make a mistake, and we will nail him.

Tom Lawrence is losing patience. He got excited when we got the name Smithson, and told Director Mueller that we would shortly have our guy. Since Smithson managed to slip through our nets, Lawrence is looking like he doesn't know what he is doing - and so of course I'm being blamed by Tom for not getting on the North Carolina connection sooner. Lawrence told me yesterday that we need to wrap this one up pretty quickly, or else "some heads may roll." I'm guessing he means mine.

I'm on the case 24/7, with the exception of the few minutes every day that I stop to call Julie.

Last week, when she got out of the hospital, we rode back to the townhouse in silence. Her Mom was waiting for us there.

Just as we turned into our garage, Julie said, "Bill, I'm going back to Waco with Mom. She can help me recuperate, and you are tied up with this case. And, I really need to think about our relationship. I'm not sure where we are going any more. I love you, but I'm not sure I can live with you when you are this obsessed."

I was stunned. "But I thought your Mom was going to stay with you here until you were feeling better?"

That probably wasn't the answer she wanted. She was gone four hours later, on a plane to Texas. I miss her desperately, but there wasn't anything I could do to change her mind. She doesn't have much to say when I call her. I know she is pretty depressed after losing the baby, and maybe she needs some psychological help to get over that - but I don't want to suggest that just yet. Right now all I can do is offer whatever help I can, and to let her know that I still love her. But when I say, "I love you," all she says back is, "I know." I'm not hearing her say it back to me like she used to every day. With her in Waco, I've been on the road a lot. I don't like staying by myself at our townhouse in Alexandria. Everything I see there reminds me of her, and I miss her that much more. If I can catch this guy and end this, I can take some leave, go be with her, and try and put our marriage back together.

The longer Julie and I are apart, the more I hate this guy.

I got into an argument today with Bill Erickson, the reporter I've been stuck with. He hasn't really done anything wrong, just straight up reporting on the team, and the fact that Julie was one of the victims of the Ricin poisoning.

He said something today, just jokingly, about how "In the good ol' days, the FBI would have had this guy strung up by now."

I jumped all over him, for no good reason. I told him that I didn't appreciate criticism of my team, even implied, from a guy who was just one step up from a video recorder.

I said, "If you want real access to this team, you have to contribute. Come up with one idea, one method, one possibility that we haven't already followed up on, and I will make you a full member of this group. And you can write anything you want about us, too. Can you handle that? Do you like a challenge?"

Bill said, "I can handle that. You might be surprised."

I shook my head and walked off. I don't need "help" from people that like to play Monday morning quarterback.

I drove home today past Arlington National Cemetery. Julie and I were last there for the Easter Sunrise Service back in April. It was cold then, and seeing the rows of graves in the snow was always a sobering and deeply moving experience. Seeing the graves through the fence as I drove by now reminded me for some reason of Robert Smithson Junior's father. I wondered how things would have been different if Colonel Smithson had survived his tour in Iraq, and come back home to a well-deserved retirement. Would something else have set off Smithson Junior? Or would he still be on the path to a PhD, and ended up helping the world through research on some disease? That one bomb in Iraq had set off a chain reaction that was still reverberating here in the United States, and there was no telling how many people would end up getting killed by the domino effects of that original bomb.

Chapter 5

James Smith
Journal Entry
Friday, October 6, 2006

Robert Smithson has been identified, so as far as I'm concerned, he no longer exists. I am now red headed, wearing lifts to make me look taller, using brown contact lenses, and I'm clean shaven again. I am at a Doubletree Hotel on the northern outskirts of Atlanta, driving a used car that I bought under my new assumed identity in Raleigh. I don't think I will ever make a payment on this vehicle, but it is possible that "James Smith" may survive this campaign, and end up with a mortgage and 3 kids in the suburbs.

Smithson's name has been released, along with pictures in every paper in the country. Even my old roommate is in trouble, because I used his name on my job application at the caterer's. I'll try and apologize to him somewhere down the line. When I left my apartment that last morning, I took a shuttle bus from UNC to the "Park and Ride" center, where you can catch a commuter bus to Raleigh. It was cool enough that I was able to wear a hoodie without anyone noticing anything strange about how I was dressed, and that kept my face from any cameras that might have been used to help trace my escape route. In Raleigh I walked about a mile, and then took a taxi to a used car dealer that I had already selected. I had already checked the available vehicles on the Internet, and knew the car I wanted. It didn't take long, because James Smith has a great credit rating. An hour later, I was on the road.

I did write a letter to Bill Peterson at the FBI, telling him I was sorry about his wife, and them losing their baby. The story of the FBI's lead investigator's wife and unborn child being personally hit by my attack on the State Department was in the papers everywhere. I told him in the letter that it was too bad that his wife had to work for an intellectual fascist like Condoleezza Rice, and that I really had nothing against Mrs. Peterson. Since my name has been in the press, I knew that Peterson would know my entire background. That would mean that he would know about my dad, and would understand what was driving me to attack our government. But I wanted him to also understand that just because my former name had been identified, nothing would change. The attacks would continue until our foreign policy changed. Apparently Peterson released my letter to the press, because the day after he would have received the letter the headlines were all about how I had promised that the attacks would continue. That was supposed to be news? They should have already known that! So much for trying to communicate with Peterson. All his reaction did was make me more determined to succeed. If he gets in my way, he will be going down, too. In fact, I am tempted to send him one of the presents that I am mailing out now.

I have spent the last two days driving the suburbs in the Atlanta area, dropping small parcels into blue corner mailboxes a few at a time. A big mailing all at once would be suspicious, so I spread it out, and mailed everything on different days, so that all the packages should arrive at their various destinations around the country tomorrow, Saturday, if the Post Office meets its own service standards for Priority Mail. I used Priority Mail because the Postal Service uses their biological agent sniffers only on letters - at this time packages are allowed to go through the system without any sort of check to see if they contain poisons or bioweapons. Only packages being mailed into the Washington area are checked for poisons and toxins - the rest of the country has their letters checked, but they are on their own as far as packages are concerned. So this time, I mailed everything to home addresses, and avoided any addresses in the D.C. area.

I would like to thank the "Dookies" for contributing to the cause. Our schools, Duke and The University of North Carolina, are rivals, including the people in the respective graduate programs. We all want to find the magic bullet that wins the next Nobel Prize. While we do compete, we do talk, and we love to brag about what we are discovering. The security on the Duke Campus is no better than what we have at

North Carolina. I have been to enough seminars over there to make some acquaintances, and getting a tour of the right lab there was no problem at all. Then it is just a matter of a small distraction, and "borrowing" a container from the lab refrigerator. I thought the Blue Devil decal on the refrigerator door in the Duke lab was a nice touch - I thought about taking that, too. Once back in my lab, I had to handle the virus material I had stolen safely, grow more of the bug in sealed Petri dishes, and then package it without getting exposed to the stuff. I tweaked the genes in this one, too, so that current inoculations and antibodies will not stop my version of this virus.

I read in the paper that President Bush has proposed legislation to make it more difficult for university and private labs to get access to and be able to work with potentially dangerous viruses and poisons. He says that security levels have to be increased ten-fold. It is too late to do any good in my situation, because all of my weapons are already prepared and in place, stashed in various places around the country, waiting on me to retrieve them. The new law will make it more difficult for others to do the research that is needed to find antidotes and cures for some of these diseases, but overall the proposed legislation is probably a good idea. If I could get away with what I've been able to do, others could manage it, too - and sometimes it is not a great idea to let these genies out of the bottle. It will be interesting to see how the legislation progresses, and how strict the rules are when the laws are actually written. I can see the educational establishment screaming about big brother, but maybe a little oversight on some of these bugs is not a bad idea. I don't know who would enforce the rules - perhaps the NIH or some other organization could perform annual audits of labs, or some such control could be built into the new law. Perhaps this unintended consequence of my actions can result in another good thing when all is said and done! And if I am captured, perhaps I can lend my expertise on how to stop these WMDs from being a security nightmare - just like hackers are now helping the government learn to properly protect their computers.

These packages, the "presents" I'm sending, are probably the most ingenious of my plagues. I spent a couple of months buying small bottles of perfume and cologne. I purchased Giorgio Armani's "Sensi" 3.4 oz. perfume bottles, and "Mania," another Armani product that is a great smelling cologne for men. I wanted a fairly costly product, because who can resist spraying an expensive bottle of perfume or cologne when you first get a new bottle, just to see what it smells like? I spread my purchases throughout North Carolina, and also Virginia and Maryland while I was in the D.C. area, so that no one would get suspicious about the amount of perfume being purchased in any one location. The Armani marketing people may be congratulating themselves on the great selling job they did in the Mid-Atlantic States!

I completely cleaned out the bottles, even going so far as to sterilize them in the autoclave in the lab. I made sure the labels on the bottles were undamaged, by covering the labels while the bottles were being cleaned. I rerigged the spraying mechanism so that once the button is pushed down for a sample whiff, the bottle continues to spray until the contents are emptied into the air. That took a simple locking mechanism on each bottle, to lock the spray button in the "open" position as soon as the button is pushed. Each bottle is pressurized, with enough juice to fill a 2,000 square ft. room. Anyone in that room will be infected, especially if they are dumb enough to stay in the room when the "perfume" starts vaporizing - and after the stubborn will I have seen from the Republicans in Congress, I believe that some of them are that dumb! I even left a little perfume aroma mixed in with my bug spray, just to help throw off suspicion while the bottle was emptying. It wasn't fun working under a chemical hood with a vapor vacuum for that length of time, with most of the work having to be done at night. But if the results mean that our boys come home earlier, the time spent making these weapons will be well worth the effort.

I bought the small bottles of each type of perfume because the entire package has to be under 16 ounces. Anything over that weight, and the packages have to be mailed at a Post Office. The Federal Aviation Administration believes that it will take a minimum of 16 ounces of explosives to bring down a plane. So, any mail that is going to fly (which means in most cases any mail piece that is traveling over 500 miles or so), and that weighs over 16 ounces, has to either be presented to a window clerk at a Post Office, or be picked up by a Postal carrier at a "known mailer." The idea is to stop a bomber from dropping a bomb into a blue collection box somewhere in the country. If you bring a package into a Post Office to be mailed, there is a good chance that either your picture is being taken, or else you could be identified by the clerk behind the counter.

Since I didn't want to be on film while mailing packages all over the Atlanta area, I made up my own small packages, and kept them under 10 ounces. That way I could use the blue collection boxes that the Postal Service conveniently scatters all over town. I spread my mailing out so that no single mail collector would be getting too many of my "presents." I knew they would all end up on the automated parcel machine at the Atlanta Airmail Facility at Hartsfield, but the machine handles so many thousands of packages an hour that my 300 or so will not be noticed - especially spread out over a couple of days.

When I was preparing these parcels, back in August, I used Stamps.com to prepare the postage label for each package. Stamps.com is a web application that allows a business or an individual to order postage online, as long as you know the correct postage for the object being mailed. I used a credit card to pay for the postage that shows the name Randy Billingsley. Apparently Mr. Billingsley had lived in my apartment in Carrboro before I did. So when I got a piece of junk mail addressed to him, asking him to send in for a new credit card, I filled out the info and sent it in. Identity theft is easy. The hard part is getting away with it over a long period of time. I wasn't going to use his credit card much - I did use it to rent the rooms I used in D.C. earlier this summer and fall. This was the last time I was going to use his credit card, and by using this card I made sure my real name was not linked in any way to the postage transaction. I didn't want to give the FBI any more clues than I had to! After receiving the credit card, I opened a PO Box using Mr. Billingsley's name at the local Mailboxes R Us, and gave that firm a fake home address. I then had the credit card company's address for Billingsley changed to the PO Box address. That way the card could not be traced back to my apartment address without some good back checking. I knew the FBI would get to me sooner or later, but I wanted to hold them off until I completed my God-appointed task.

Getting that credit card was so easy that I repeated the process under several more names, using different PO Box addresses. Lots of people in my apartment complex throw away their "junk mail" in a trash can right by our mailboxes. All I had to do is pull out the credit card applications, change the address slightly, and I had another card. I now have extra cards to use each time I attack, so that the FBI will not have the name I am using at the time. They may know my face, but with a little luck I should be able to operate incognito under my fake names until this is over.

I used the Republican National Committee's address on First St SE in Washington as the return address on each package. Making fake labels on the computer takes no effort at all. I thought that using a known return address would get a few more of these packages opened, as Republicans are used to getting mail from that organization. I only targeted Republicans this time around - they are the majority party in both houses of Congress, so they have quashed any attempt to pass legislation to set a timetable for getting our troops out of Iraq. Preparing sealed packages for 55 senators and 230 representatives took 10 days to prepare, which took up a lot of my time in August. Each seven ounce package cost $4.05 to mail. I wonder if I can deduct that expense from my income taxes this year?

I also sent out my usual warning letters. You would think that our political leaders would start to realize that I am serious about this. We will see how many people I have to kill before we see a change in attitude in D.C. I started this

119

journal with a Shakespeare quote about a "pox on both their houses." Maybe "boil, boil, toil and trouble" should apply to Congress, too. I know the Macbeth quote is actually "Double, double, toil and trouble," but I like the often misquoted version better. Nothing like a few boils to get people moving faster...

Bill Peterson
FBI Headquarters
2:22 PM Saturday October 7, 2006

This time it was Smallpox, but a version the National Institute of Health had not previously seen. How did this guy get access to all of these diseases? We were again pretty fortunate to stop this one before it got too far. If nothing else, his attacks have been good tests for our infectious disease security system! We got the warning letters this morning, and then when the packages started being opened, it didn't take long before word got back to Homeland Security, and then to us. We intercepted most of the packages before they could be delivered. It looks like only about 40 actually got opened, and we think only 68 people were possibly directly infected. We are giving vaccinations to around 250 more people that came in contact with the possibly infected individuals and the packages before we could get them into quarantine. Most of those were at either a campaign breakfast at Senator Kay Bailey Hutchison's home in Houston, Texas, or at a brunch at the home of Senator George Allen in Virginia. 22 of the people exposed were actually members of Congress - 4 senators and 18 representatives. 20 of those are running for reelection. Do you know how tough it is going to be to keep them away from everyone else for the next two weeks, during the incubation period for this disease? Once you are directly exposed to the virus, it is too late for a vaccination. So we will just have to wait and see if the people exposed to the disease actually come down with it. Since normally the infection is absorbed through the lungs, and they were all breathing what came out of the perfume bottles, there is a good chance that most of these people will actually become ill with the disease. Senator Hutchinson is a good friend of the President, and she has already called Mark Sullivan asking when we will stop this guy. Sometimes it is better not to be the guy in charge!

I would expect there will be a sympathy vote for those that were infected - and it will be interesting to see what happens on November 7th. There has been a lot of media stir about people that support the war being voted out of office. Now Smithson is trying to subjugate that political process, and take matters into his own hands. How people will handle the terror campaign and their own feelings toward troops in Iraq will be worth watching. We got copies of the usual threatening letter:

A WARNING TO THE COUNTRY'S POLITICAL
LEADERSHIP

YOU DID NOT HEED MY FIRST THREE
WARNINGS. SO, JUST AS GOD (THROUGH
MOSES) SENT A PLAGUE OF BOILS INTO
EGYPT, I HAVE USED BOILS TO REMIND
THOSE THAT HELP MAKE THE LAWS THAT
SHAPE OUR FOREIGN POLICY THAT YOU
NEED TO CHANGE YOUR WAYS. THOSE OF
YOU THAT MAKE THOSE LAWS SHOULD
TAKE HEED, AND INSURE THAT THE
PROCESS TO BRING HOME THE COALITION
TROOPS BEGINS QUICKLY. THIS TIME IT IS
DISEASE. THOSE THAT THOUGHT THEY
WERE RECEIVING A GIFT WHILE FAILING TO
DO THE PEOPLE'S WILL MAY BECOME
DEATHLY ILL. SOME WILL DIE. PERHAPS

122

WHILE YOU ARE ILL YOU SHOULD CONSIDER YOUR ROLE IN STOPPING LEGISLATION THAT WOULD HAVE SET CONCRETE DATES FOR BRINGING THE TROOPS HOME. AS YOU DID NOT START THE PROCESS TO PULL THE AMERICAN TROOPS OUT OF IRAQ BEFORE THE END OF THIS CONGRESSIONAL TERM, YOU WILL PAY. NOW A SPECIAL TERM ELECTION WILL BE NECESSARY, TO ELECT SOMEONE TO DO WHAT YOU SHOULD HAVE ALREADY DONE. AS MOSES SAID TO THE EGYPTIANS, "LET MY PEOPLE GO!" IT TOOK THE PHARAOH TEN PLAGUES BEFORE HE LEARNED. HOW LONG WILL IT TAKE YOU? IS FOUR ENOUGH, OR DO I HAVE TO STRIKE AGAIN, AND AGAIN, AND AGAIN? WILL IT

TAKE SEVEN TIMES SEVEN? IF PROGRESS IS NOT SEEN RAPIDLY, MORE PLAGUES AND PESTILENCE WILL RAIN DOWN UPON YOU, JUST AS DISCUSSED IN THE BOOK OF EXODUS. START THINGS MOVING TOWARD TOTAL WITHDRAWAL, OR YOUR DAYS ARE NUMBERED!

Our pshrink guys think the repetition of the numbers ten, and seven times seven, might have more of a meaning to our guy than just quotes out of the Bible. They are speculating that he might have seven plagues planned, or ten to match what Moses used the first time around, or 49. They predict the future about as well as I predict the winner against the spread when my Redskins are playing the Cowboys. I wish I had time to actually watch a game live, instead of having to just catch the highlights on Sunday nights on ESPN.

I do see an escalation in attempted violence. Smithson has gone from burning cars to actually killing diplomats to trying to kill over half of our senators and representatives in Congress. Mr. Sullivan thinks the same, and has doubled the agents on both the President and Vice

President. Who else Smithson is after, and what stunts he may pull next, are anybody's guess - but we are going to try and be as prepared as possible.

We've traced the postage he used on the packages, but that was another dead end. The private Post Office box business has been great for criminals of all stripes, from drug dealers to porn distributors. They have been a thorn in the FBI's side since they first started getting popular back in the '80's.

The Postal Inspectors are trying to determine where the packages were mailed, but so far no luck there. This guy is making us look like fools. Tom Lawrence has been making more and more pointed comments about our lack of progress. His "assistance" consists of veiled threats and comments like "time is of the essence." The fact that we identified the guy on just a minimum amount of evidence seems to have totally escaped his memory. Smithson is still on the loose, so according to Lawrence I haven't been doing my job.

Congress is about ready to dismantle the entire Homeland Security Agency, and start over with another agency that they think "might get something done." Some right-wing Congressmen are telling President Bush that he should declare martial law, and suspend the Bill of Rights, until we catch this guy. I wouldn't want to be caught sneaking around the Capital dome in the near future!

We are starting to get "copycat" people wanting to get in on the action. A waiter at a Georgetown restaurant put ground glass in the dishes for a Congressman and a lobbyist meeting for dinner. In Chicago, a woman sprayed Mace into the face of Congressman Henry Hyde as he was out trolling for votes. She shouted "This is for Moses" as she let him have it.

A guy at the University of Nebraska started selling t-shirts with "What Would Moses Do?" on the front, and "What Weapons of Mass Destruction?" on the back - both with the WMDs emphasized. The picture on the shirts show the Washington monument, with a mushroom shaped cloud in the background. He is making a mint selling then on the Internet. I don't know how to handle the positive reaction from some people to Smithson. He is a serious criminal, a terrorist, and a murderer - but some sick people are giving him folk hero status. I'm hoping no one is actually helping this guy, just because they think he is some sort of modern crusader, tweaking the establishment. This isn't some hippy from the '60's staging a sit-in at some government office to protest the war in Vietnam. This guy is killing people. Some people apparently can't tell the difference.

The entire country is starting to panic. There have been complaints about the Post Office not inspecting every piece of mail before it is delivered. They handle millions of pieces of mail a day! Are people willing to pay a dollar for a stamp, just to make sure their mail doesn't include something that might kill them? This is the same public that for years wouldn't pay for the airbag option when buying a new car - most people felt the extra security wasn't worth the extra cost, until there was legislation requiring the bags on every car.

And the smallpox perfume bottles were sealed tightly enough that even a machine or animal sniffing for biological agents might not have caught the problem. Some marketing firm announced that online perfume sales had dropped over 20% since this attack. Now Smithson is starting to affect the economy! These attacks lead almost every newscast these days. This guy has certainly succeeded in getting his platform out there in front of the public. I can't tell that he has swayed anyone's opinion on the war, but everyone knows how he feels!

Julie is still in Waco. I still call her, but I feel she has somehow changed, and maybe the thought of me when I call reminds her of her loss. She hasn't invited me to come see her, and I haven't asked lately. Our phone conversations consist of a lot of too-long silences, with neither of us speaking, but neither of us wanting to hang up. She tells me that she is fine physically, but still pretty depressed. I really can't blame her. I am too - but at least I have an outlet for my emotions, trying to catch Smithson. I don't know if I could handle just sitting around thinking about what might have been all day, as she is obviously doing. I wish I could be there with her, but what I'm doing is important, and I don't know anyone who could take my place - so I need to stay the course, at least for now.

Sally has asked me twice to come to her place for dinner - she says I deserve a home cooked meal. She knows that I have been surviving on fast food and TV dinners - not the most nutritious fare, and guaranteed to make you have to loosen your belt. I've always prided myself on staying in good shape, but now I'm beginning to wonder why. I may take her up on her offer, just to get something decent to eat.

FBI Headquarters
7:30 PM Friday October 20, 2006

We have 33 people in the hospital with Smallpox. We have two confirmed deaths, and 20 more people listed in critical condition. A few more of the really old Congressmen may die, and there is one 72 year old secretary that opened the mail in Tennessee that is in pretty bad shape. She couldn't resist smelling her boss' perfume. Again, no epidemic, and the attempt at killing off Republican members of Congress seems to have failed for the most part.

We checked all the labs at the University of North Carolina, and none were working with this particular disease - but we did find a lab just down the road a few miles at Duke that was still keeping samples of the virus on hand. They were not supposed to have it at the Duke Medical Center, but scientists and professors apparently think they can do what they want when it comes to their pet bugs. We're guessing that Smithson somehow got access to the Duke lab (those grad students often do exchange visits between universities), and stole the Smallpox sample. His credit cards show no purchases for the perfume or cologne bottles, so either he paid cash, or used a card in someone else's name. We checked out the card he used to buy the postage for the Smallpox packages, but there were no retail purchases on that card. We are using an NSA Cray computer to review all credit card purchases within 500 miles of Raleigh over the last six months, to see if we can find a pattern of perfume purchases on a single card. This might give us the name he is now using, or it might just tell us the names of all the guys with more than one girlfriend. If the ACLU knew we were reviewing all the credit card purchase records, they would be screaming about another invasion of privacy. We don't care what they think. We want this guy hung by his toes, and if we have to step on a few toes to get the evidence that stops him, so be it. One good thing about having driven him away from his lab is that he can't prepare any more surprises. He may still have some things stashed away, to be used in the future, but unless he has access to another lab somewhere, we've at least managed to slow him down. We do have people tracking lab equipment purchases, just to make sure he doesn't try and set up his own lab at some out of the way location.

Sally and I spent all afternoon yesterday at Postal Service Headquarters in L'Enfant Plaza, working with the Postal Inspectors. They have identified Atlanta as the mailing point for the Smallpox packages. We don't know if our guy is still in the Atlanta area, but we have agents watching all the rental car agencies, the airports, bus stations, train station, and so on. We're not leaving any chance to catch this guy go by without a serious attempt to apprehend him. After our meeting, Sally and I ate at the Chinese restaurant on the ground floor of L'Enfant with a couple of the Inspectors, and then moved over to the Plaza hotel's pub for a drink. She told me she had finally dumped the semi-boyfriend.

She said, "Wally is history. I think you were right about Aggies preferring sheep."

I almost choked on my drink.

She said, "I don't have time for a boyfriend, anyway, with as much time as we are putting in on this case."

She asked how Julie was doing, and I said, "Well, things aren't the greatest. We still talk, but she's still not happy with me, or what I'm doing. She still seems a bit depressed over losing the baby. I need to be there with her, but I'm also needed here. Someday I guess I'm going to have to decide between her and the Bureau."

Sally agreed that relationships are difficult when you are working 70 - 80 hours per week.

We left the bar, and she took my arm and leaned against me as we walked the few blocks back to FBI Headquarters. We didn't talk during the walk, but it felt like there was an invitation there somewhere to continue the evening. I thought about it for a second, but I didn't follow up on it. Besides, I was dead tired, and needed my 4 hours of sleep. Lawrence is still on my butt, and even though I don't need him to motivate me, I would like to catch this guy just to get Tom to shut up.

Chapter 6

James Smith
Journal Entry
Monday, October 30, 2006

I'm back in the Washington area, ready to press forward again. I'm getting frustrated. The medical people have gotten lucky, and saved most of the people that have been exposed to my bugs. None of my previous attacks have seemed to move people to start thinking about getting our troops out as soon as I would like. The President is even talking about sending MORE troops over there, to help train more Iraqi security forces - and that only after those local people are trained could we look at reducing our force level in that country. He claims that this "surge" of additional troops will actually help to shorten the war. He is still talking years!

I'm going ahead with my Halloween party favors, and it looks like my November plagues are going to be necessary after all. If I succeed in all three additional attacks, it may be enough to bring down our entire political system. Plus, it is only another week until the midterm elections. There is enough sentiment out there in my favor to possibly swing the balance of power in both houses of Congress over to the Democratic side - and maybe then things will start moving. But I can't count on the electoral process, so I'm staying busy. My message to the establishment will reflect my attitude - no more esoteric ramblings. Now it will be simple and direct - get our boys (and now, girls) home, or you may die.

I have nothing at all against the Pentagon. It is not our soldiers' fault that they have been sent, once again, into harm's way. But the Secretary of Defense is another matter. He is not a soldier, but a political animal with an ego the size of Rhode Island. At the American Legion's national convention, he said critics of the Iraqi occupation were "...trying to appease a new type of fascism." Rumsfeld said that critics of the United States' policies have "moral and intellectual confusion," and said that such critics are afraid to fight back. I'm not afraid to fight back, and the SecDef is my next target. Earlier this year, eight retired generals asked that Rumsfeld resign. They said that his inability to foresee the instability that the war in Iraq would cause, his lack of planning for a post-war strategy, and his refusal to admit that he made a mistake and now should change policies were enough reasons that he should leave office. Of course he refused, and the President backed him. I personally think the generals were right, and it is time for Donnie to move on. I'm going to see if I can help him do just that.

The social pages of the Washington Post have been all atwitter about the Halloween gala being thrown at Rumsfeld's home on Kalorama Road in Washington. Kalorama is an exclusive subdivision off of Dupont Circle, right next to what is known as "Embassy Row." Birdseye, Rumsfeld's place, is worth about $3.5 million, give or take a few hundred thousand bucks. Not bad for a guy that made it through Princeton on a scholarship, and flew jets for the Navy for a couple of years. He made the big bucks when his drug company came out with Aspartame, the sugar substitute. I hope he enjoys white powder - I'm going to send him some that I grew just in his honor.

You can buy almost anything online these days, including Halloween masks of almost any political figure. At a company called Costume Craze you can buy masks of Condi Rice, the President, Schwarzenegger, Hillary Clinton, almost anyone you want - including Donald Rumsfeld. A dozen Rumsfeld masks set me back about $260, including shipping. These are high quality masks, with a removable inside liner - which comes in handy for what I have in mind. A little powder between the liner and the mask doesn't appear to be out of place. Perhaps that is there just to make it easy to pull the liner out, or perhaps it is part of the manufacturing process. No one will mind a little powder - until it kills you. Cheap at the price of $19.69 each. And who can resist wearing a mask on Halloween? Especially if the mask is a spitting image of the master of the house? I can see the Visa commercial on television now: Halloween party, $20,000; Halloween masks, $260; Killing the Secretary of Defense? Priceless!

134

I assumed that any Postal package would be vigorously inspected after my last stunt, so I decided on UPS for this delivery. I had the package prepared well in advance, including a sealed liner on the inside of the box, so that none of the spores could escape before the package was opened. I started to copy the name, address, and logo of the Costume Studio on 8th St NE for the return address on the package, but I had a better idea. I ordered myself something from that costume shop, and then reused the return address part of the label that they sent me. That made it look more official. Rumsfeld's address was easy to find on the Internet. All the war protesters know it - they held an anti-war rally in his front yard a few months ago.

I slapped my preprinted address form on the package, filled out the UPS shipping paperwork with the usual fake info, taped a $20 bill to the front to cover postage, and dropped it next to the UPS collection box outside of the mail store on Pennsylvania Av NW. That way I didn't have to actually go into the shop, and get my picture taken on their video camera. One reason I picked this particular UPS mail drop is that there did not appear to be any cameras on that block of Pennsylvania - no ATMs or banks, no jewelry stores, or other places where security cameras are commonly used. I knew the FBI would eventually trace the package back to that UPS store, and I wanted to avoid pictures of me or my car being available for review by the feds.

The people that run those stores are usually minimum wage employees. Unless someone was really sharp, nothing suspicious would be noted about my package. I assumed that whoever took it into the store would rate it up for postage, and then just pocket the change out of the $20. I was parked across the street, so I just fed the parking meter, and sat in my car. I pretended to read a book and looked like I was waiting for someone, but I actually watched the shop. Sure enough, at noon a guy came out, emptied the collection box, and took all the packages and envelopes back inside. I didn't see any cops or Secret Service types show up in the next couple of hours, so I was pretty confident the package would be delivered on Halloween at the Rumsfeld's - just in time for their party. The package is sealed well enough that it should get past any checking for bugs that UPS performs prior to delivery. Trick or treat, everybody. Party on, Donnie boy.

Bill Peterson
FBI Headquarters
9:22 AM, Saturday, November 4, 2006

Another 12 people in the hospital. 48 more on Cipro. A stronger warning message. I wish we still had the old west "Wanted: Dead or Alive" list, so that we can shoot on sight. It was Anthrax this time around, coated inside of costume masks that looked like Donald Rumsfeld, delivered on Halloween to the Secretary of Defense's home here in Washington. We had no idea that Moses had struck again until the people that actually wore the masks started showing up with flu-like symptoms yesterday. We think we have everyone out of danger, and no one will die from this attack. It was close, again. Donald Rumsfeld is in the hospital, in fair condition. He couldn't resist putting on one of the masks - he thought it was a great joke when he came home to the party, and everyone that met him at the door looked just like him. He tried one of the masks, and look where it got him. He told Mark Sullivan that if we can find this guy, he will call out the National Guard to help us make sure he doesn't get away again.

According to Mark, the Secretary's parting comment was something like, "Putting an M-48 round up his ass will really make my day."

The warning was received this morning, almost too late to save some of this scumbag's potential victims. I really think he is planning the delivery of these warnings so that it is too late to save some people.

A WARNING TO THE COUNTRY'S POLITICAL LEADERSHIP

YOU DID NOT HEED MY FIRST FOUR WARNINGS. SO, JUST AS GOD (THROUGH MOSES) SENT A PLAGUE OF LIVESTOCK DISEASE INTO EGYPT, I HAVE USED A LIVESTOCK DISEASE TO REMIND THOSE THAT CONTROL THE AMERICAN TROOP DEPLOYMENT THAT THERE IS A CHOICE. THOSE OF YOU THAT CAN MAKE THE DECISION TO BRING THE AMERICAN TROOPS HOME, BUT HAVE NOT DONE SO, MUST NOW BE REPLACED. THIS DISEASE CAN BE DEADLY. IF YOU WERE LUCKY, AND THIS DID NOT KILL YOU, DO NOT THINK YOU ARE NOW SAFE. AS MOSES SAID TO THE

EGYPTIANS, "LET MY PEOPLE GO!" IT TOOK THE PHARAOH TEN PLAGUES BEFORE HE LEARNED. HOW LONG WILL IT TAKE YOU? IS FIVE ENOUGH, OR DO I HAVE TO STRIKE AGAIN, AND AGAIN, AND AGAIN? WILL IT TAKE SEVEN TIMES SEVEN? IF PROGRESS IS NOT SEEN RAPIDLY, MORE PLAGUES AND PESTILENCE WILL RAIN DOWN UPON YOU, JUST AS DISCUSSED IN THE BOOK OF EXODUS. START THINGS MOVING TOWARD TOTAL WITHDRAWAL, OR YOUR DAYS ARE NUMBERED!

That sounds pretty clear to me. Either we catch this guy, or he will continue to strike. I don't know how many more tricks he has up his sleeve, but so far he has shown he can be pretty creative. There are a lot of us on the task force that have started reading our Bible more regularly, trying to get ahead of this madman. We have tracked down every credit card in every name he has used to help buy equipment or to ship his WMDs. If any of those cards show up on anyone's computer, anywhere in the country, we will be instantly notified. We are going so far as to check every car that we recorded on our cameras traveling north or south on I-95, or on the Beltway, with a North Carolina license plate. We are backtracking, and checking the names of the owners of every one of those cars. If the guy bought another car in North Carolina under an assumed name, and put a North Carolina plate on that car, we will get that name. That will take a while, but we are the FBI. We never give up!

Sally has asked me again to come to her apartment for dinner. I told her I would when I could find the time. She wanted to pin me down to a date, so I promised her I would come sometime in the next two weeks. I'm not sure where this is leading. I'm confused about my relationship with Julie, if I still have a relationship, and I don't know how to handle my budding feelings about Sally. She has been more than just an assistant for security issues on this case. She can think out of the box. What I don't know is what she really thinks about me. I still call Julie on a regular basis, but distance is definitely not making the heart grow fonder, at least that's the way it looks in her case. I miss her, but I am tied up in this case, and don't really have time to think about my personal life. Maybe when this is over, I can straighten out my own life. All I can do now is put everything personal on hold, and hope I still have a life to go back to when this case is over. When I ask Julie if she wants to talk about losing the baby, or about us, she says it is too soon, and changes the subject. She is sounding more and more distant every time we talk.

I woke up this morning in my lounger, still sitting in front of the TV where I sat down last night to eat my Taco Bell dinner. I was so tired that I fell asleep in the chair after finishing off my tacos. I slept there all night, not even waking when ESPN switched from SportsCenter to Texas Hold 'Um poker reruns. The TV was still running, showing the morning version of SportsCenter when I finally opened my eyes. The crick in my neck today is not so much from tension over the case as it is my poor night's sleep. I tried both a hot and cold shower, but nothing seemed to get me fully awake. I need a break, but I can't afford one. The country needs my team to succeed, before pure panic ruins everyone's life.

I dreamed last night that I was named manager of a minor league baseball team in South Texas. Is my subconscious trying to tell me that I need to dump this job and go be with my wife? Or find something less stressful to occupy my time? I'm not sure if the dream meant anything. It could even be something less obvious, like Smithson plays a lot of baseball. Or maybe somewhere deep in my mind I always wanted to coach. I have no idea.

Bill Erickson did an op-ed piece for the Post yesterday that made it sound like Smithson is public enemy number one. He talked about how political change is sometimes brought about by revolution, but that almost always occurs only when the entire populace rises up against a tyrannical regime. One person killing politicians, with others dying as collateral damage in the wake of the attacks, is not a revolution but simply terror. And terror is a crime that should be severely punished. Erickson spent a good bit of time in the column reviewing Smithson's "accomplishments" to date - the number that have died, the turmoil this terrorist has caused, and the fear under which a lot of people are now living. And no one is basing their feelings on the Iraqi war on what Smithson is doing. It's like Smithson is the one operating in a vacuum, the same crime he accuses the politicians of committing.

Erickson went on to say that anyone abetting Smithson should be punished just as strongly as Smithson will be punished when he is caught. Terror is not heroic under any circumstances. Bill noted that "What Would Moses Do?" t-shirt wearers should be ashamed of the clothes on their back, and everyone else around them should tell them that until they take the shirt off. Erickson added that everyone should be on the lookout for Smithson, and that he would probably be found from a tip from some sharp eyed member of the public. Maybe I was wrong about Erickson. I like the spin he is putting on this, even if we still seem to constantly be a step behind our perp. Erickson may prove to be useful yet - but he still hasn't really done anything concrete to help us find Smithson.

I told him I liked his column. He said, "If we can get enough people to realize what Smithson is doing to the country, we can have millions helping us to find him. He couldn't last long out there with the entire country helping to track him down."

Not a bad sentiment. And I liked how he said "we." Maybe he is thinking that he is a part of the team, and not just a neutral observer. I want him on our side.

Of the people on Moses' mailing list, the only people he has not tried to hit are the President and Vice President. I don't know what is coming, but I have a strong feeling it will be aimed at one of them. The plagues from the Book of Exodus that are left - gnats, locusts, darkness, and so on, don't make literal sense in this day and time. But this guy will not quit coming at us until we put him down.

The entire country is sitting, waiting with baited breath, to see what he will try next. The media circus on this has made him bigger than any rock star out there. The election on Tuesday may give the Democrats back control of Congress, and this guy may actually get some version of what he wants, and disappear. But I will spend the rest of my life looking for him

143

anyway. He may think he is Moses, but I'm going to be the devil that either puts him either on his knees, or sends him to face his real maker. And if it takes me 40 years of wandering to get him, so be it.

James Smith
Journal Entry
Saturday, November 4, 2006

I couldn't find anyone on the UNC campus working with Anthrax, so I had to head back south, to my old stomping grounds in Gainesville, Florida. The University of Florida has a big veterinary school right next to the main campus, along with a law school, medical school, and all the other graduate programs that go with a state's flagship university. Florida is the second leading beef producing state in the United States, behind only Texas. Anthrax is often found in cattle hides, and is always being studied at UF.

I had to work a little to get access to the bugs. My old ID was still good for the lab I used to work in at the McKnight Brain Institute at Florida, before I got my BA degree. But that ID would not get me into the vet labs. I borrowed a white coat I found hanging behind a door, a clipboard, and just acted like I knew what I was doing and that I was supposed to be in the Vet school. I pretended to be doing safety checks of the labs. I told the veterinary students that opened the lab doors when I knocked that I was checking safety protocols on alleged cross-contamination issues between labs that had been phoned in anonymously as a potential safety hazard. I knew that some professor would finally call the Dean's office to check on me, but I thought that if I could get in and out of there fast enough, I could pull off the culture theft. I hit the labs early in the morning, sure that the grad students doing research would be there, but also pretty sure that the professors would not - most of them don't make the scene until 9:30 or 10:00, unless they have to teach an early class. Sure enough, in the second lab I visited, there were sealed cultures of anthrax in their refrigerated storage area. I slipped one of the agar containers into my lab coat pocket, made my exit, and I was out of Gainesville, on I-75 headed back north, twenty minutes later.

Working with anthrax is pretty easy, as long as you are careful. A few cells can be multiplied into a lethal dose within a very short time frame. The spores are actually brown or gray in color, and not white. The press and their emphasis on "white powder" got it wrong as usual. The spores are so small that the white powder the terrorist mixed in with the bacteria is the only thing that can be seen. The talcum powder is used as a transport medium, to help spread the spores into the air when an envelope is opened, or in the case of the Post Office, when it goes through a pinch point on a conveyor belt in their sorting machinery. The spores were simple to grow, as they multiply exponentially in a blood/protein culture. Then all I had to do was dry them, transfer them to the inside of each Halloween mask, and then replace the liner in the mask. I started to bake the spores onto each mask, but my experiments showed that the loose powder in the mask would stay in place just about as well when the liner was put back into the mask, and the loose spores would be easier to inhale. Anyone wearing one of the masks would be breathing in enough spores to infect them within a few seconds. Of course, all of this handling of the bacteria and the masks had to be done under a vent hood, to prevent me from getting infected, and to prevent the spores from spreading across the rest of my lab at UNC. All this was obviously completed before I had to abandon the lab. The finished masks had to be sealed in an airtight container to keep the spores from escaping into the air as I moved the masks to Washington. I'm not trying to kill my lab partners, and I'm not trying to commit suicide with my bugs.

There are cures for anthrax. Strong antibiotics taken right after exposure, or before symptoms get too severe, will usually stop the disease. I'm hoping that Rumsfeld just thinks he caught the flu, and doesn't go in for treatment until it is too late to save him. Just 24 hours too late in getting treated, and the disease is nearly 100% lethal. I don't care about the rest of the party goers. They are probably sycophants and other Rumsfeld toadies that deserve the same penalty that I am imposing on Donnie boy. He is one of the main reasons my dad was in Iraq, and Rumsfeld needs to pay the penalty for not only the decision to go to war, but his idiotic post-war strategy that has cost us so many lives. Wanting to make a few extra bucks for his buddies in the oil business is no reason to get American soldiers killed in a war we have no business fighting.

James Smith
Journal Entry
Wednesday, November 8, 2006

The elections yesterday were a disappointment. The Democrats took the majority in the House, and it looks like they might have a 51-49 majority in the Senate, if the Republicans don't win recounts in a couple of states where the voting totals are pretty close. With the Democrats only controlling small majorities in each chamber of Congress, very little will get accomplished in the next two years. That leaves control to the Executive Branch of the government, because the President can veto anything that comes out of Congress on the war, and the Democrats don't have enough of a majority to override a veto. If Bush and his cronies feel that protecting their oil interests means that we need to stay in Iraq, then we will stay in Iraq, and Congress will not be able to stop them. Dick Cheney has already been quoted as saying, "We're going to stay the course in Iraq. Our policy will not change due to this election." Therefore I have to keep moving forward. I may be the country's last and best hope to get us out of this war.

I read what Bill Erickson said about me in the Washington Post, and all I can say is that he doesn't understand me at all. This is not simply about terror. It is about revenge for taking my dad away from me and my family. Francis Bacon said, "A man that studieth revenge keeps his own wounds green." I know that time would help heal the wound that still sticks in my heart - the untimely and unnecessary death of my dad. But I am bound on revenge, so I cannot take the time to let myself heal. Once the troops are headed home, I can make peace with the idea that my dad will not be coming back. But until then, on with the show.

One of the things that helped to get us out of Vietnam were the televised shots of coffins being unloaded in San Francisco, showing the returning dead soldiers from another unjust war. Vietnam was the first war to be televised, and the true horror of war came across pretty well on the small screen. I don't know if people have just gotten jaded due to all the violence they now see on TV and the movie screen, or if American soldiers getting killed overseas now just seems to be old hat. Somehow I've got to get people back to realizing the horror that those pictures from Vietnam generated. What happened to all of those anti-war hippies from the '60's? I need them marching in the streets one more time!

Chapter 7

James Smith
Journal Entry
Wednesday November 15, 2006

This weekend I will bring darkness, another plague from Exodus. Close to the sad anniversary of John Kennedy's assassination, I am working to bring down another pillar of our government. Things will start moving more rapidly now. If this warning does not get some immediate positive results toward getting people out of Iraq, I will be forced to make my strongest, and hopefully my final attack. I know that God is guiding me, and I cannot fail. Yet it is hard when I don't see the results that I want to see. I know that God has a bigger picture that we cannot comprehend, but I felt from the beginning that my mission would prevail. I have to keep faith that the promise of success is still out there. I have that strong trait of stubbornness that will not let me give up. However, I do keep remembering the words of W.C. Fields, "If at first you don't succeed, try, try again. Then quit. No use being a damn fool about it."

I'm cold, and I can see my breath. I know how to survive in this weather, and I'm properly dressed for it, but I don't like it. Maybe this will work, and having to be miserable while I set up this particular operation will have been worth the effort. Snow is fine, when you are sitting in front of a warm fire, with something warm to drink, watching the snow fall outside your window. But walking and working in this stuff is no fun. I've known how to ski since I was a kid, and that can be fun at times. But wearing snowshoes and trying to walk in new powder, or breaking a new trail on cross country skis is a lot of work. The sacrifices I make to help my country!

Every time I work with this explosive I keep hearing Jimmy Walker, playing the character JJ on the "Good Times" TV show, with his, "Dyn-O-Myte!" Those old TV shows somehow stick in your head, and pop up at the strangest times.

Making dynamite is pretty easy, once you understand the formula, and if you have access to the chemicals needed. I had actually started preparing the nitroglycerin, the explosive part of dynamite, when I made my first scouting trip to Colorado this past June. To make dynamite, you mix nitro with diatomaceous earth, which can be purchased at any pool supply store. Diatomaceous earth is used in pool filters to filter impurities out of the pool water. It is also the inert substance that keeps nitroglycerin from being too sensitive. Nitro in its pure form can be exploded just by a sharp movement of the substance, and that is why there were so many explosive injuries prior to Alfred Nobel finding a way to make nitroglycerin safer. His mixing of nitro with diatomaceous earth made him his fortune.

The problem with dynamite is that it can be *too* safe. It takes a pretty strong blasting cap to set it off. Making an electric blasting cap (I needed an electric cap so that I could use a timer) is more difficult than preparing the dynamite itself. Blasting caps can be made, too, using fulminate of mercury. And I was prepared to make those, too. I was going to do whatever I needed to do to pull off every one of my plagues. If I had to make dynamite and blasting caps, then I would take the time to do so.

But what I found when I got to Colorado on the reconnaissance for this part of my mission was that the Colorado Department of Transportation crams 100% of their road repair work into the three months of good weather they have in that state. As I approached the Eisenhower tunnel on Interstate 70, coming west out of Denver where I had spent the night, there were a lot of construction signs, including signs asking that all radios, cell-phones, and walkie-talkies be turned off due to blasting. I decided this play merited further review, as they say on pro football games. I turned around at the next exit on the Interstate, and headed back east. I looked for a hotel room in Silver Plume, the closest town east of the pass, but couldn't find anything. I was forced to go a few miles further east, back to Georgetown, to find a place to stay.

I took a hike that afternoon, to scope out the construction site. What I found was about what I expected. Using binoculars to search the site from atop a nearby mountain, I located a locked shed, marked "Caution: explosives," and a lot of road grading material and machinery. There did not seem to be a fence for a dog, or a trailer for a night-time guard. This was out in the middle of nowhere, in the high mountains. No one in their right mind would be bothering the construction site out there, or at least that appeared to be the thinking of the construction company. That night I went back, prepared for a little B&E burglary work. I didn't want to bust the lock off the front door of the shed, so I took a battery powered portable screwdriver with me (along with a crowbar, just in case). I unscrewed one panel on the side of the shed using my screwdriver, pulled it open, and voila - all the explosives and blasting caps I could possibly need. Again, I didn't want my presence noticed if at all possible, so I took one box of dynamite from the back of the shed, and I grabbed just enough blasting caps so that they wouldn't be missed - only taking a couple from each box. I put all the other boxes back the way I found them, with the exception of one box of a different type explosive - that one was so unexpected that I grabbed the entire box. I was hoping that the loss of the explosives would not be discovered for weeks, if at all. I screwed the shed side panel back on, and hiked back to where I had parked my car. I grabbed my shovel, and buried the explosives in a waterproof box at the base of a big tree, where I could find them when I returned, just a short hike from where I had parked in a pull-off-the-road observation point/rest area on the west-bound side of I-70.

I know that explosive inventories have to be taken and reported back up the line from any blasting site on a regular basis, but I also know that at a site where a lot of blasting is taking place that inventory counts are not always as accurate as they should be - and I hoped that would play to my advantage. The worst scenario would be a "missing explosives" alert going out the next day after my burglary, and some Colorado Highway patrolman remembering my car parked the night of the crime at the scenic overlook approaching the pass. I never did see anything on the missing explosives on any Colorado news Internet site, so it looks like I got away clean.

Now it is November, and the climate has changed a bit here in the high mountain country. There is now about 10 inches of snow on the ground, and it is about fifty degrees cooler than when I was here in June. I've already recovered my buried explosives. All I had to do was wait until nightfall, hike a hundred yards from the scenic overlook where I had parked before, and dig up my box. It was cold, miserable work, but I got it done. There weren't any cars at the overlook when I parked, and none there when I returned. It gives me a visceral thrill to know I have the power to move mountains stored in the trunk of my car. I don't know how God brought darkness to Egypt. That could have been fog, an eclipse, something that sucked up all available light - who knows what God used to create his miracle. Anything is possible when miracles are involved. I'm a little more practical. When you want to turn out the lights, you go to the source. That is much easier these days than it was in Biblical times. All you have to find now is your friendly mountain town power plant or electrical relay station. Once again, the Internet and Google Maps comes through, and I am on my way.

I mailed my latest warning letters this morning from Denver. I know they will not be delivered for a couple of days in Washington at best, and probably not delivered until Saturday. I don't think I was specific enough in my letter that they can tie it to Colorado before the fact, so even if some of the letters get delivered a day early it will not make any difference. This time I tried to get even firmer:

A WARNING TO THE COUNTRY'S POLITICAL LEADERSHIP

YOU HAVE NOT HEEDED MY EARLIER

WARNINGS. SO, JUST AS GOD (THROUGH

MOSES) SENT A PLAGUE OF DARKNESS

INTO EGYPT, I WILL BRING DARKNESS TO

YOU. THOSE OF YOU THAT CAN MAKE THE

DECISION TO BRING THE AMERICAN

TROOPS HOME, BUT HAVE NOT DONE SO, MUST NOW BE REPLACED. THE DARKNESS I BRING WILL CAUSE SUFFERING, AND POSSIBLY DEATH. IF THIS DOES NOT KILL YOU, DO NOT THINK YOU ARE NOW SAFE. AS MOSES SAID TO THE EGYPTIANS, "LET MY PEOPLE GO!" IT TOOK THE PHARAOH TEN PLAGUES BEFORE HE LEARNED. HOW LONG WILL IT TAKE YOU? IS SIX ENOUGH, OR DO I HAVE TO STRIKE AGAIN, AND AGAIN, AND AGAIN? WILL IT TAKE SEVEN TIMES SEVEN? IF PROGRESS IS NOT SEEN RAPIDLY, MORE PLAGUES AND PESTILENCE WILL RAIN DOWN UPON YOU, JUST AS DISCUSSED IN THE BOOK OF EXODUS. WHY SHOULD THE AMERICAN PEOPLE SUFFER

FOR YOUR STUBBORNNESS? IF YOU

CONTINUE TO ABUSE YOUR POWER, AND

MAKE DECISIONS IN A VACUUM, YOU

DESERVE TO LOSE POWER. MAKE THE

POLICY CHANGE! START THINGS MOVING

TOWARD TOTAL WITHDRAWAL, OR YOUR

DAYS ARE NUMBERED!

Some people just can't get away from their roots. Apparently once you have worked for Halliburton you are a member of that family for life. Or at least until "death and stock options do us part." I'm in Colorado to see if I can't help that separation occur a little quicker than planned for some people. Dick Cheney is partying at the Halliburton CEO's place in Vail. If I bring a plague of darkness to that town, will Cheney learn to really separate himself from his old buddies at the construction conglomerate? Will it help him realize that he needs to start working to get us out of Iraq? Am I getting anywhere? Is *anyone* listening? Sometimes I wonder. This plague reminds me of the old Simon and Garfunkle song -

Slip sliding away, slip sliding away

You know the nearer your destination, the more you slip sliding away.

Or a better tune might be, "Turn out the Lights, the Party's Over...."

Bill Peterson
Ronald Reagan National Airport
9:35 AM Saturday, November 18, 2006

Dick Cheney, the 46th Vice-President of the United States, was assassinated last night. He actually died of a heart attack, induced when the home he was staying in was demolished by an avalanche. Vice-President Cheney was visiting David Lesar, the current CEO of Halliburton, at Lesar's vacation home in Vail, Colorado. Lesar was Cheney's hand-picked successor at Halliburton when Cheney resigned the CEO post to run for Vice-President on the ticket with George Bush back in 2000.

Yesterday was the opening day of the Vail Ski Resort, and Lesar always hosts his friends at his home for that opening. The avalanche was no accident. This was Smithson, again. He somehow planted explosives on Vail Mountain, high above the town, and set off the avalanche right at 4 AM. My guess is that he thought even the late night partiers would be home by that time of the night. According to the warning letters received this morning (a day late, of course), his goal was to bury the power station in Vail, darkening the entire town. He did do that. He also shut down Interstate Highway 70 through that area, so rescuers cannot get by road from the airport in Eagle into Vail.

The avalanche set by our perp did what he wanted it to do - leave the town without power. What he wasn't counting on (or maybe he was, I'm not sure) was that his avalanche set off sympathetic vibrations on a slope overlooking Lesar's home, and that entire neighborhood suffered severe damage when the snow on that mountainside let loose as a second avalanche.

There are 16 people dead besides the VP, and 12 more that we know of are still listed as missing, buried somewhere in the debris and snow. Two Secret Service agents, on Cheney's protection detail, are among the missing. Lesar survived the attack, but he does have a broken leg.

Lesar's home was right on the side of the mountain. It probably had a spectacular view, but when the top of the mountain came down on the site there was nothing in the way to stop the snow, rocks, and trees from tearing right through the house, and those of the neighbors around it.

We have road blocks on all the roads leading out of the area, and we are checking every room in every condo and hotel, but of course no sign of Smithson. Vail still has no power, which is limiting our communication capabilities with the area. The FBI did helicopter in a few agents from my team, along with some ATF explosive experts, but very little information has been sent back to us here in Washington so far this morning.

It is officially no longer my problem. I was relieved yesterday afternoon, before this latest attack occurred, from my Team Leader position. Tom Lawrence claimed that he was under pressure from the Director to show some success at catching Smithson, and since we had not made any progress since the smallpox attacks that I had to go. My suspicion is that it was either Lawrence's neck or my neck on the line, and he took the easy way out. I don't really blame him if he is telling the truth - I would have probably done the same thing myself. He has now taken direct control, and is personally running what was my team.

And I guess the fact that I was no longer her boss was the excuse my conscience needed to allow me to keep my dinner date at Sally's apartment last night. She had been after me for weeks to let her fix me a home cooked meal, and I guess I needed a shoulder to cry on after Lawrence finished debriefing me.

I arrived at her door with a bottle of an '82 Merlot that I liked, and wondering just what the evening held in store. She opened the door in a full length apron, and what looked like something pretty expensive, short and sleek, underneath.

She gave me a peck on the cheek as a welcome, took my coat and the wine from me, and led me into her kitchen. I sat on a stool and admired her cooking while she finished preparing stuffed veal, sweet potatoes, and fresh green beans. The smells reminded me of my days in my mom's kitchen back in Texas. Of course, like a lot of Texans, we were staunch Southern Baptists. So we weren't sipping a glass of wine, waiting on dinner, while I was growing up!

Sally lit a couple of candles, took off her apron to show off a fabulous dress (that highlighted every curve), and we sat down to what was without doubt the best meal I had eaten in months. She knew what Tom had done to me, so we resolved to talk about everything but work during dinner. We touched on everything, including normally verboten subjects like politics and religion. We didn't notice the time, but between the great food and the conversation, we sat there for nearly two hours.

It was nice just to have a normal conversation. My evenings had gotten into a routine of a frozen dinner or fast food, a beer, and the 11 PM SportsCenter on ESPN - the only vice left in my life. I hadn't even seen a single full quarter of a football game on TV all fall, something that I normally looked forward to as much as the holiday season. I finally realized that I was enjoying myself because I was comfortable being around Sally. I helped her get the dishes into the dishwasher, and she brought coffee into

161

her living room. She put some soft jazz on her stereo, and sat down beside me on the couch. I don't know if it was the wine, the atmosphere, or what, but the next thing she had snuggled up against me, looked up at me, and leaned in toward me. So I kissed her.

On the tip of her nose. I pulled back, and saw the look on her face that had to be a combination of confusion and desire. I took her hands in mine.

"I hope that didn't give you the wrong idea. I like you a lot, but one, you are too young for me. Two, you work for me, or at least did, and three, I'm married to a wonderful woman, whom I'm on my way to go see now that I've been relieved. If we started something, somewhere down the line I would break it off to run back to Julie, and you would get hurt. Besides, from what you say about being kissed by Wally, I don't think I can compete!

She laughed, and said, "And one more thing - I know you're in great shape for your age, and I know you sometimes still run 10Ks on weekends, but if I jumped your bones, it would probably cause your heart to give out. And the team still needs you if we are going to find Smithson."

I took a deep breath, just to try and get my brain back in gear. I definitely wasn't used to a woman like this one!

"OK," I said, trying to gain back control of the situation, and to keep us both from being embarrassed in any more ways. "We're probably right on all counts." We both laughed again. Even though I was feeling pretty foolish, and Sally had given me a bit of a guilty conscience to boot, I really didn't want to leave. I realized that I really did enjoy just sitting and talking with her! I decided the best course of action was to change subjects.

I said, "I apologize if I came across giving you the wrong ideas, and maybe we both made some illogical assumptions. So maybe like the old song from the White Stripes, I can tell we're destined to just be friends. And I do appreciate what you are saying about needing me to help catch Smithson. I'm not really sure you do need my help, because it is obvious that you are a lot smarter than I am, considering how well you have thought through this manhunt so far. I do want to know one thing, though. Speaking of how smart you are, tell me what it was like growing up a child genius?"

She looked thoughtful for a moment, and then a little sad. "It was like I was always out of place, like a kid that has wandered into an adult party. I was always socially maladjusted, because I had no one my age I could talk to at school. My folks tried to find me playmates when I was younger, but the other kids wanted to play dolls or dig in the dirt, and I wanted to play Space Invaders or solve crossword puzzles. My parents finally gave up, and just let me be. It was lonely at times, especially when I got to college. A fake ID wouldn't do me any good when I was 13, so

163

drinking with my classmates was out. And I wasn't invited to too many parties, either. I ended up taking 21 credit hours a semester, and testing to place out of another 3 courses or so. I didn't have time to do much but study and write papers.

Georgetown Law was much better. We had study groups, and I could hold my own there, because I was respected for my knowledge - my age didn't matter. I wasn't going to be asked out, but at least I was being treated as an equal in class by the other students, and I really enjoyed having some interaction with other people. The professors there dumped on me just like everyone else. Either you knew the cites for the cases we were studying, or you didn't. There was very little middle ground, and I excel in that atmosphere. There were other people there that were pretty smart, too, so I didn't stand out as much, except for my age.

Once I got through law school, the NSA was fun for me. Breaking code is now mostly done by computers, but someone has to program the machines, to tell them what to look for. That was my job, and I've always loved solving puzzles. I still can't talk much about what I did there, but it was important work, and I enjoyed it. But ever since I was a little girl, and saw Efrem Zimbalist, Jr., playing an FBI agent, that's all I ever wanted to be. That's why I went to law school in the first place, and that's why I'm here. One day I'm going to be Director. And I know that I will be accused of sleeping my way to the top by everyone that I bypass along the way, but I will know that it is not true, and that is important to me. And that's another reason I'm not going to sleep with you, if that is what you thought was going to happen when I invited you over. Now, let's get down to business. How are we going to get around Lawrence, and keep you in the loop on what our team is up to? I know you are officially out of power, but we all know we couldn't survive without you. What are your plans, and more importantly to the team, what are we going to do now?"

I was thankful that she still wanted me to stay involved with the team. "Does the rest of the team feel the same way? That they want me to stay in the loop?"

She assured me that they did. I told her my plans, and we made arrangements to keep in touch. I grabbed my coat, and hugged her before I walked out.

"Thanks for a great dinner. And if there is anything I can do to help you make Director, let me know."

Sally laughed, and said, "You're welcome. And remember that we still want you to help guide us in our hunt for this monster. We know how capable you are, even if Lawrence refuses to recognize that fact."

All the way back to my place all I could say to myself was, "You idiot! You really could have had some fun with that girl, and you blew it!" But then I changed my mind. Would anything really have occurred, even if I had kissed her properly? She's so smart that she's been three steps ahead of me since the team was formed. I'm pretty sure she would have found a way to defuse the situation even if I had made a pass.

And that's why I'm at the airport, instead of working on the case. I'm flying to Waco, Texas, half-way between Dallas and Austin. I don't care if my wife wants me there, because I'm going anyway. I've got to do something to see if I can save my marriage. Besides, President Bush will be in Crawford next week for Thanksgiving, after the Cheney funeral. And the President is the only one on Smithson's list that hasn't been hit. I may not be the nominal head of my team, and officially I'm on leave, but I will never give up looking for Smithson.

James Smith
Journal Entry
Sunday November 19, 2006

I skied Vail on Friday, doing the tough upper mountain downhill slopes early when the lifts first opened, to sharpen my rusty skiing skills, and then spending the early afternoon doing cross country runs around the bowls on the back side of Vail Mountain. I already knew where the power station for the town was located from my scouting trip this past summer, so I had a pretty good idea where I would want to place my explosives. The skiing was just to verify how things looked under a blanket of snow, to see how the ridge lines had changed when the snow built up, and to check access and egress routes for my next move. The ski patrol people were busy with the usual idiots that thought a half day of ski school qualified them for a black diamond run. They were tied up having to haul out a lot of injured people, so they were not paying any attention to those of us that seemed to know what we were doing. I only saw two other people on the back trails, and no one from the ski patrol. If the Secret Service had anyone on duty that knew how to ski, they were staying away from the top of the mountain. I left early, before the lifts closed and the parties and drinking started, and headed west to Beaver Creek, just a couple of miles down the highway. It gets dark this time of year early in the mountains. I had a condo there under another assumed name and credit card, one that I had not used before, and I hoped the FBI had not stumbled onto that name. The place I was staying advertised that you could ski right from your front door, and I planned on using that to my advantage.

The tough job was getting back up the mountain from my condo at the base of the hill. I had thought about just hiding somewhere in the back country on Friday afternoon until it was time to plant my toys, but the ski resort people were good about keeping track of how many people went out skiing cross country, and how many came back in. I had to check back in by Friday afternoon, or else the ski patrol would have been out all night Friday night looking for me. I had also thought about using a snowmobile to help me get back to the elevation where I wanted to be, but the noise would have alerted people in Vail. So I had to climb using my own muscles, and climb I did.

I started out about six PM, as soon as it was dark, and skied cross-country back to Vail. It took me nearly 4 hours to get back up to the area where I wanted to lay the charges. While climbing, I had my skis, my backpack holding my bombs, and a shovel strapped to my back. I was wearing snowshoes, and with all the heavy clothing on I felt like I was carrying 250 pounds up the side of that mountain. But I made it. Out of breath, sweating under my clothes (which was not good), and not sure if there would be any guards out after dark, I took a long time to get to my blasting point. I couldn't use a flashlight, because that would have been seen from Vail, too. When I got to my designated blast location, I had to dig through the snow, force a hole into the frozen ground deep enough to hold the dynamite and my other explosives, and set the timers for my charges. I used three different locations for the charges, all set to go off at the same time. With digital timers, you can get blast ignition times synchronized down to the second.

I knew it would not take me long to get back down the mountain, even skiing without a light, because there was enough moonlight to see where I was going. So I set the timers for 4 AM, put my skis on, and pushed off. I took it easy skiing back down the mountain. I couldn't afford a fall and a broken leg with the mountain about to chase me down the hill! I was back at the Condo by 2:00 Saturday morning, dead tired, but I kept moving and I was on the road 20 minutes later. By the time the charges went off, I was through Denver, and headed south on Interstate 25 towards Raton Pass, then into New Mexico, and eventually towards Texas. I stopped and slept a little in a small motel just south of the Colorado/New Mexico state border, and took my time heading southeast through the Texas panhandle. I got into Austin this afternoon.

There has been some talk since the election about how Bush, as a conciliatory move, fired Rumsfeld (no one believed that Rumsfeld really tendered his resignation on his own). That would have been a good first move toward getting us out of Iraq. However, with Cheney now dead, there is already speculation that the President might name Rumsfeld as Vice President! I find it ironic that I tried so hard to kill Rumsfeld, but got Cheney instead. Back under Reagan, Cheney was Rumsfeld's protégé. Rumsfeld brought Cheney into the inner circle. There is talk that Rumsfeld thought that when Bush II first sewed up the Republican Presidential nomination that he, Donald H., might be Bush's choice for VP, and that Rumsfeld was very disappointed when Cheney got the call instead. The student had surpassed the teacher. I'm sure it didn't hurt that Cheney was in charge of the VP search committee. Now because of my actions, Rumsfeld may get the post after all.

Other prognosticators are leaning toward Condi Rice. I would prefer her over Rumsfeld, just because she is smarter. I find it amazing that the same group that got us into this mess keep getting recycled into other jobs, instead of being sent packing. "The more things change, the more they stay the same." This old French proverb was quoted by George Bernard Shaw's *Revolutionist Handbook* in 1903. That is an apt source, considering that I am trying to bring about a revolution of sorts. But real change still eludes me, so I will continue tilting at my God-given windmills.

George W. is next on my list of people that need to suffer. It is time for the Bush family to be touched by this war first hand. Perhaps that is what it will take to make him realize what this war is really doing to families all over America. Sometimes I think he feels that he is just managing another baseball team, like the days when he was part owner of the Texas Rangers. If you need a few more players, just have them shipped in from the minor leagues - or in this case, the National Guard. Bush is handling this mess in Iraq like it is just another game, and that strategy has to end quickly. Until one of my plagues can show him the error of his ways, he will continue to wander down his own personal yellow brick road, with a scarecrow Condi and Tin Man Rumsfeld dancing by his side. I'm pretty sure the Wizard died in Vail in the avalanche. Have a happy Thanksgiving, Mr. President.

Bill Peterson
Waco, TX
10:45 PM Sunday, November 19, 2006

Julie and I are back together, sort of. She seemed glad to see me when I got out of the car at her Mom's house yesterday. I flew into Dallas, rented a car, and drove south down I-35 to Waco. Waco is a college town, built around Baylor University. Julie did her undergraduate work at Baylor before coming further south for grad work in Austin, and to meet me while I was at the University of Texas Law School. While I was at UT Law, she was doing graduate studies at the LBJ School of Public Affairs.

Baylor is a Baptist school, and Waco is called "Jerusalem on the Brazos" because of Baylor, and not because David Koresh and the Branch Dravidians decided to make Waco their headquarters. That was not one of the FBI's finest moments, as Margaret, Julie's Mom, reminds me at every opportunity. The Brazos River runs through Waco, and right through the Baylor campus.

People that went to Baylor are some of the most ardent fans of their school that I have ever seen. They seem to stay friends for life, mostly

171

marry each other, and are always looking for excuses to come back to some function at the school. I'm surprised Julie agreed to marry someone that didn't go to Baylor. I told her when we started dating that I had played baseball against the Bears in Waco in my undergraduate days, and I guess that was close enough. We were married in her home church, the First Baptist Church here in Waco.

When I got there, no one was home. So I sat out front in my rental car and started going through the emails that had collected while I was flying and driving. Julie and her Mom pulled into their driveway about 20 minutes later. They had obviously been out shopping. Julie gave me a big hug, holding on to me with dear life for what seemed like a long time. Her Mom was less gracious. "What are you doing here?" was her fairly rude welcome. I told her, "My wife needed me, and I needed my wife. So here I am." Margaret just shook her head and headed for the house. I thought I heard her murmur, "About time." Julie stayed with me while I unloaded my suitcase, and helped me unpack in Margaret's spare bedroom. As I hung up my clothes next to hers, Julie kept looking at me like I had been gone for years. I finally sat down on the bed next to her, took her hands, and looked into her eyes. "I am here because you need me. I apologize for not being here sooner. And if you will forgive me for that, I'll try to be a better husband than I've

172

been." Julie just smiled, and gave me another hug.

She slept with me last night, but we didn't make love. I'm not sure just how comfortable she is with me being here. When she invited me to go to church this morning, with her and her Mom, I took it as a good sign. The First Baptist Church here in Waco is huge. The church has several Sunday morning services so that there is room for everyone that wants to come. We attended the eleven AM service, with Dr. R. Scott Walker, the lead pastor at the church, giving the sermon. He is one of the most dynamic speakers I have ever heard, so I didn't mind sitting through one of his services. I expected a Thanksgiving sermon, since this coming Thursday is Turkey Day, but apparently he saves that for Wednesday evening, Thanksgiving eve.

Today he gave more of a pre-Christmas advent sermon, speaking on the signs and portents in the Bible predicting Jesus' birth. He talked about how several Old Testament prophets predicted a Savior was coming, to be born in Nazareth, and how Elizabeth, a relative of Mary's, became pregnant several months before Mary. According to the Book of Luke, Elizabeth's child, John the Baptist, leaped in Liz' womb when he heard Mary's voice. John was the first born of Elizabeth, who had been barren until she was supposed to be too old to have children - but God made it happen, so that John could help pave the

173

way for Jesus. I was just happy to be hearing about some part of the Bible besides Exodus!

The three of us, Julie, her Mom, and I, all went out for lunch after church at the El Chico Mexican food place on the circle in Waco. That place has been there for at least 40 years, and sometimes you wonder if the refried beans have been there that long, too. But you can't get Tex-Mex in Washington like they make in Texas. I was happy to get a chance to eat there, even if it was just a chain restaurant's normal menu. Julie's Mom offered to let us be alone for lunch, but we both wanted her to be there with us. Julie's Dad died when she was a little girl, and her Mom raised Julie, all by herself. Julie turned out to be a smart, independent woman. Even in the short time that I had been there I could tell that Julie had leaned on her Mom a lot to help Julie get through the loss of the baby. I wish I could have helped more, but maybe there was still a chance that we could work things out between us. Margaret talked at lunch about all the things they had done since Julie got home - going to Baylor football games (they are actually winning a few games now - when Julie was in school here they consistently won about one game a year), concerts on campus (but no dancing in the aisles - not allowed at a Baptist school!), and shopping trips to the nearby outlet malls. Julie was pretty quiet, content to let her Mom lead the conversation. I listened to Margaret rattle on, but a part of my mind was still on the sermon from

174

this morning. Something had struck a chord, but I couldn't quite put the pieces together. I left it simmering in my subconscious, sure that it would come to me after another night's sleep.

When we got back from church, Julie and I sat down in the swing on Margaret's front porch. I wanted to explain to Julie what had happened to me at work. I told her, "I was relieved on Friday. Tom Lawrence told me we haven't done enough to capture Smithson, and he and his bosses want the team 'going in a different direction.' I don't know where I'll be assigned when we get back after our vacation."

Julie said, "Anywhere will be fine. I'm not ready to go back to the State Department after what happened to me at that dinner in September. I'm sorry they didn't give you a chance to finish this - I know how much capturing Smithson has meant to you, because of what he did to us personally, and how hard you've worked on this case."

Julie and I talked a little, in generalities, about how the last few months had altered our ideas of what our futures might bring. Career changes, family changes, all sorts of things can change in an instant. She told me, "You know I love you, but I didn't love what you had become - a workaholic obsessed with making AD, no matter how many hours you had to put in to get another notch in your gun. And after being poisoned and me losing the baby, you still didn't seem to understand how much I needed you

175

around right then. So maybe you getting relieved will work out in the end for the two of us, even if you see it right now as a setback."

Julie kissed me hard when we went to bed, holding me tight. I touched her face, but when my hand started to wander a little lower on her body she grabbed my hand and stopped me.

She said, "Wait. I'm just not ready yet. You'll have to be patient."

What could I say? If patience is what she wants, patience she will get.

Chapter 8

James Smith
Journal Entry
Wednesday, November 23, 2006

I really wanted to build a dirty bomb for what I'm calling my "Bush Basher." I had even started lifting a few radioactive cartridges from the UNC Medical Center back in the spring, hoping to make a radiological dispersal device, what the Nuclear Regulatory Commission calls an "RDD." These bombs are not really nuclear weapons, but simply powerful explosives with radioactive material included in the bomb, so that when the bomb goes off, radioactivity is spread over a large area. However, nuclear physics is not my field of expertise, and the more I studied the subject, the more I realized how difficult it would be to collect enough radioactive material to make a difference in my bomb. Unless you have access to some left over sludge from a nuclear reactor, it would take hundreds of pounds of the stuff used in hospitals and construction sites to have enough radioactive material to really contaminate a large area. The British Ministry of Defense did a study that showed that high explosives alone would cause more of a problem than a mix of high explosives and radioactive material, unless something like U_{235} is used in the bomb. To build a true Radiological Dispersal Device would require me to somehow obtain stuff that true terrorists are having trouble getting their hands on. My dad had told me that he had seen a study stating that Iran and North Korea were working on potential RDD "dirty bombs," and that was one reason that they had been labeled as terrorist states.

What really changed my mind about trying to build a dirty bomb was the second surprise from my summer visit to the Colorado construction site. Mixed in with the dynamite were several boxes of Semtex-A. Semtex is an older form of plastic explosive, made originally in Czechoslovakia. Distribution of the explosive is usually pretty well controlled by the manufacturer and downstream distributors, because just a little of it can bring down a plane. When the Transportation Security Agency people check your shoes after you go through the metal detector at the airport, they are looking for plastic explosives in the heels - just like what Richard Reid tried to use on that American Airlines flight from Paris to Miami. His main explosive was PETN, one of the main ingredients in Semtex.

I guess the Colorado road construction people thought they might have some really big rocks to pulverize, because they had several boxes of the big blast explosive stored in the back of the shed. I took an entire box of the stuff - a dozen bricks. Each box of Semtex in the shed was full, so I thought a missing brick might stand out more than a missing box. The extra 12 pounds in my backpack didn't slow me down much at all, but I did have a random scary thought as I was hiking back to where I was going to bury the explosives. If I was to slip and fall on my backpack, the resulting explosion might show up on the earthquake monitors at the University of Colorado in Boulder.

I used one brick of Semtex in each of the three holes I dug to start the avalanche on Vail Mountain, and that might have been a tad too much firepower. I'm assuming the huge explosions that I caused, trying to take out the Vail power plant, were the reason for the secondary avalanche that ended up killing the Vice President.

The room I'm planning on emptying out for my next trick is about the size of a large living room, and will probably be holding twenty-five to thirty people at the time. That's no problem for a few ounces of Semtex!

Bill Peterson
Waco, Texas
4:25 PM Wednesday, November 23, 2006

Thank God for cell phones. Tom Lawrence may think he is running my team, but the rest of the team keeps me informed through phone calls, so that I am always up to date. Almost everyone on the team is staying in McGregor, Texas - just west of Waco where I am, and close to the President's ranch outside of Crawford.

We got Smithson's latest warning letter today, so we know that the President is the next intended victim of our perp. We know that the ATF forensic people found traces of Semtex in the holes left by Smithson when he caused the avalanches in Colorado, so we know he has access to plastic explosives.

We also think we have identified the car he is now driving. He used another assumed name while in Colorado, but we found his fingerprints at a condo in Beaver Creek, after searching about two hundred empty condos where people had fled after the explosions. The condo rental agency there have a security video camera filming everyone that drives up to the rental agency to pick up their keys. He is (or at least was) driving a 2007 metallic blue Honda Accord Coupe. We assume it is a rental, because it would have been difficult for him to buy a new car with one of his fake names. We are running down the list of all rented Hondas in the entire United States, with an APB out for that car. All of the law enforcement people in this area have been notified to watch for that car, but we haven't released a description to the press yet. We want a chance to catch him before we let him know his car is "hot." We didn't get a license plate off of the video, so any Honda within 50 miles of Crawford, Texas stands a good chance of being stopped by a cop. I hope a deputy sheriff doesn't shoot some Sunday driver by mistake.

Smithson is getting bolder in his messages, basically telling now ahead of time what he is going to do, and daring us to stop him. This time he wrote:

A WARNING TO THE COUNTRY'S POLITICAL LEADERSHIP

YOU HAVE NOT HEEDED MY EARLIER WARNINGS. SO, JUST AS GOD (THROUGH MOSES) SENT MANY PLAGUES INTO EGYPT, I WILL BRING MORE PLAGUES TO YOU. THIS MESSAGE IS FOR THE ONE THAT HAS THE ULTIMATE DECISION MAKING POWER ABOUT BRINGING THE AMERICAN TROOPS HOME, BUT HAS NOT DONE SO. I BRING SUFFERING, AND POSSIBLY DEATH, TO THOSE THAT OPPOSE MY WISHES. AS MOSES SAID TO THE EGYPTIANS, "LET MY PEOPLE GO!" IT TOOK THE PHARAOH TEN PLAGUES BEFORE HE LEARNED. HOW LONG

WILL IT TAKE YOU? IS SEVEN ENOUGH, OR DO I HAVE TO STRIKE AGAIN, AND AGAIN, AND AGAIN? WILL IT TAKE SEVEN TIMES SEVEN? IF PROGRESS IS NOT SEEN RAPIDLY, MORE PLAGUES AND PESTILENCE WILL RAIN DOWN UPON YOU, JUST AS DISCUSSED IN THE BOOK OF EXODUS. WHY SHOULD THE AMERICAN PEOPLE SUFFER FOR YOUR STUBBORNNESS? IF YOU CONTINUE TO ABUSE YOUR POWER, AND MAKE DECISIONS IN A VACUUM, YOU DESERVE TO LOSE POWER, AND YOU DESERVE TO SUFFER. MAKE THE POLICY CHANGE! START THINGS MOVING TOWARD TOTAL WITHDRAWAL, OR YOUR DAYS ARE NUMBERED!

Smithson has to know that we are close on his tail, so we don't think he will wait long to strike. Plus, his history shows the attacks occur quickly after we receive his messages (if not before we receive the message). The Secret Service has basically put a steel cordon around the President, and he almost has to have signed permission just to walk outside of his home at the ranch in Crawford. The war protestors that were camping out just down the road from Bush's ranch have been cleared out as a security precaution - the Secret Service said they didn't want Smithson using the protestors as a smokescreen.

The entire Bush clan has gathered at the ranch for Thanksgiving, including George Herbert Walker Bush, the current President's dad and former President (# 41), and Jeb Bush, the outgoing Governor of Florida, and the probable Vice-Presidential nominee for the Republican Party in 2008. Everybody at the ranch has all of their kids with them, too. An atomic bomb at the ranch could wipe out our entire ruling family!

So my team is assisting the Secret Service, trying to keep that from happening. I'm planning on spending Thanksgiving with my wife and her Mom, watching some football, and sleeping off Thanksgiving dinner. I may drive over to McGregor and meet with the team on Friday, just to make sure Lawrence isn't screwing things up too badly. I want the team to succeed, with or without me.

Julie and I are going back to church tonight, for the First Baptist pre-Thanksgiving service. I'm hoping Dr. Walker's sermon will ease my mind. Sunday's sermon is still rattling around in my head. Julie and I went for a walk around the Baylor campus today. The conversation was interesting, to say the least.

She started off saying, "You know, we really weren't talking that much even before I lost the baby. When I got here, I was thinking about a divorce. You were ignoring me, obsessing over this case so much that I wasn't even seeing you, and barely hearing from you, for days at a time. A job is important, but your family has to have a place in your life, too. And after losing the baby, I really needed you - and you weren't there for me.

I responded, "I know. And I was wrong. My family has got to come first, no matter how important the case. All I can do now is apologize."

Julie interrupted me. "When I first got to Waco, I didn't want to see anyone, talk to anyone, or do anything. Mom finally got me going back to church, and I talked to Dr. Walker a couple of times about losing the baby. One Sunday night, a group of us went out for dessert after services. I started talking to Sammy Thurman, I guy I had known at Baylor. He's a widower - his wife died of cancer. We sat in the Elite Cafe off of 35 and talked and talked. He told me about his loss, and I told him about mine. When I looked up,

184

everyone else had gone, and it was just Sammy and I there. We were enjoying having someone to open up to, and before we knew it we had been there for hours. It was nice just to have someone to talk to - you know what I mean?

I nodded. "I do. I had a similar experience, talking to Sally. You don't know how much you miss a simple conversation until you have one. With me thinking about the case day and night, I wasn't really talking to you at all, and we should have been talking and sharing things all the time.

Julie cut me off, again. "I didn't finish. What I haven't told you is that when we got up to leave, Sammy asked me to come back to his house to 'continue the conversation," as he put it. I had enjoyed being with him so much, I really thought about going with him. I got as far as his car, but when he opened the car door I realized that if I got in his car, that would have shut the door on you and me. So I told him I couldn't, until I had a chance to see what was going to happen with our relationship. I got in my own car, and drove back to Mom's.

Maybe it was the loss of the baby, maybe it was because I didn't see the compassion from you I needed, whatever - but I came close to going home with another guy. All I can say now is I'm sorry, nothing really happened, and I'm glad it didn't. But I'm also saying that if we don't change how we treat each other, our relationship isn't going to make it. I want us to be together, but only if each of us makes the other the most important

185

thing in our lives. Or maybe second, behind God. But paying attention to and caring for each other has to be right up there."

I didn't know what to say. I had come close to the same thing (at least in my mind) with Sally. I had ignored my wife, putting my career and this damn terrorist ahead of everything else in my life. I had made a mess of things - ruined my relationship with my wife, probably ruined my chances of ever getting the AD job, and acted like an idiot at Sally's. I deserved to be kicked to the curb by everyone involved.

I told Julie, "You don't need to apologize for anything. All of this is my fault, for not giving you the attention you deserved, especially after the Ricin attack. But that is changing, as of now. I don't know what I'm going to be doing with the Bureau, or even if I will stay at the Bureau in any capacity. But I can guarantee that you will be my number one priority in life. If you'll give me another chance, that is. I'm the one that screwed up - not you. Will you forgive me, and help me to get us back to where we should be? I think being here, away from Washington, has helped us both see things a little more clearly. Maybe D.C. is not the place to be for us - but wherever we end up, I want us to be together."

She told me, "First Baptist has a tradition that on the Sunday closest to Valentine's Day, Dr. Walker will ask all the married couples in the congregation to stand and repeat their wedding vows. I think I would like to come back to Waco for that service next spring. What do you think of that idea?"

I couldn't think of any way of responding other than to kiss her. I do love my wife, and she loves me. Now if we can just catch Smithson, all will be right again in our world. Things can't go back the way they were, but we can always start over.

James Smith
Journal Entry
Thursday, November 24, 2006
Thanksgiving Day

I took my model plane out for one last test flight early yesterday morning, Wednesday. I have the center of gravity set perfectly, and the plane balances well, even with the extra weight in the plane. The half-pound of Semtex and the blasting cap doesn't seem to bother the plane's lifting capability at all. Of course, I didn't have the blasting cap inserted into the explosives on this test flight!

I was going to wait to finish hooking up the blasting cap until I had the plane in place at my launch point, ready for takeoff on Friday. I flew the plane out in a circling loop as far as a quarter of a mile away from where I stood, well within the range of the plane's controller. I just wanted to make sure that there was no degradation in the plane's handling when it got out some distance from the controller.

This particular model, the Hangar 9 Alpha 60 trainer, is made from lightweight aluminum instead of Balsa wood, has a six foot wingspan, and can allegedly be controlled from a distance of up to a half mile. I won't need anywhere near that amount of distance for what I have in mind. I did want the large plane, so that it could handle the extra weight I was adding, and because the larger models are much easier to fly. It is slow, because of its size and lack of power in its engine, but what I need is accuracy for where I plan on "landing" my plane. Plus, the heavier model will add extra momentum when I bring it into the target area. I've modified the model, so that I can start it from a distance using an optional remote electric starter. Otherwise someone would have to start the engine for me, and I don't want anyone helping me with this project. I was careful to make this test flight a very simple one - takeoff, fly a circle, and land gently. I don't want to just put a big crater in the runway here at the Old Settlers Aerodrome in Cedar Park, north of Austin - I have more important "fish in a barrel" in my sights. I was lucky in that there wasn't anyone around when I did my test flight Wednesday morning. A plane that big will be remembered, and I didn't want any recognition.

I dismantled the model, boxed it up, and drove downtown to the building I'm going to use as a takeoff runway. I had already scouted out access to the roof of the University of Texas Fine Arts Building, and found an overhang area on the

188

roof that will hide the model plane from prying eyes looking down from the air. The roof is just big enough to give the plane the necessary space for a takeoff roll. I wanted to get the plane in place before the holiday, because I was afraid the building would be closed for Thanksgiving.

I walked through the building, carrying my box, and everyone I saw assumed I was a student just carrying another piece of artwork. I guess you could call what I have in mind performance art - "Revenge of the Wronged" or something like that. I got to the roof stairs without any problem, cut the lock on the roof door, climbed the stairs up to the roof, put the model back together, and hooked up the starter. The model is in place, and ready to start at my signal. I put the broken lock back in place on the roof door, and hopefully anyone checking the area will not notice the broken lock until after my attack.

All the practicing I did with the plane at the model airplane field in Raleigh, back in the spring, will (I pray) pay off with a successful flight. This model uses a three servo controller box, with one running the throttle, one controlling the flaps and ailerons (tied together), and the one handling the rudder. More experienced model airplane pilots can fly using a four servo controller, but I don't need that level of control for what I have in mind. I don't expect to be doing aerial acrobatics, or engaging in combat with another model plane in my short flight plan.

I hated this Thanksgiving, the first without my dad. Our family will never be whole again. I hope President Bush enjoyed his turkey. If I succeed, this will be the last one his entire family enjoys together. I ate at a restaurant in a South Austin suburb with a lot of other misfits, strangers, and people with no place to go on a holiday. I had bought a new cell phone, and I tried to call my sister to wish her a Happy Thanksgiving. No one answered the phone at my sister's apartment. I'm guessing that they don't answer unless they recognize the name on their caller ID of the person that is calling, and I obviously couldn't program my real name into my new phone. I did write them a letter, trying to explain why I was doing what I was doing. I don't know if it will help them feel any better, but at least I was able to try and explain my motivation. I am still determined to succeed. I think my sister has better sense than to let that letter get into the papers.

The new Democratic controlled Congress may make efforts to get us out of Iraq, but if Bush is still there to veto everything that Congress sends to his desk, we will not get anywhere. Someone has to show him that there are consequences to his stubbornness. He still seems to be living in a vacuum, and doesn't realize (or doesn't care) how the American people feel. Thomas Jefferson said, "Whenever the people are well informed, they can be trusted with their own government. Whenever things get so far wrong as to attract their notice, they may be relied on to set them to rights." That is what I have been doing, and I have been making some progress. There are a lot of editorials now about time to change our Iraqi policies, and a lot of people are comparing this war to Vietnam. The one stick-in-the-mud holdup is the President. I'm going to see if I can alter his reality, and then see if our national policy does change.

Bill Peterson
Weston Inn Suites, McGregor, Texas
9:00 AM Friday, November 25, 2006

Well, we made it through Dick Cheney's funeral and Thanksgiving without Smithson (or anyone else!) taking a shot at George Bush. I'm in McGregor, about to meet with my team. I was supposed to be here at 8:00, but Julie and I didn't sleep much until the wee hours of the morning. Everything seems a little brighter this morning, but I was embarrassed to have to call the team and tell them to postpone our meeting for an hour, because I had overslept. Lawrence had stayed in Washington - I guess he felt that he wasn't needed here for the holiday. He doesn't know that I am rejoining the group, but they do need a leader. Bill Erickson is the first to see me through the motel dining room window, and waves. Everyone stands up as I approach the back room table, which makes me feel a little better about seeing them again. At least this group still respects me a little! Sally moved from the seat at the head of the table, giving me that chair. The waitress approached, and I asked for coffee. Everyone else was already just about finished eating breakfast. I was hungry, but too embarrassed to order food after being late to breakfast. Sally said that they were just bringing each other up to date on the latest on the search for Smithson. Everyone gave a report on their particular part of the investigation, but there is really not much new. Somehow we have to figure out what this guy plans for the President, and get there before it happens.

I pulled out one of the old standby management handbook techniques. "OK everybody, when you are stuck, you go back to the fundamentals. We are going to start from the beginning, and see what we've missed."

We start over with a review of the firebombing of the parking lot, what we saw on film, and the first warning letter. How the guy kept talking about God's plagues that were used in Egypt.

Erickson nodded toward the print on the wall of the motel restaurant, showing the skyline of New York. "At least Exodus didn't have any plagues about bringing down the Twin Towers. We have got to be getting close to the end of the plagues in the Bible that Smithson can relate to for his modern-day versions."

That's when it hit me. The sermon on Sunday morning had mentioned that John the

Baptist was to be Elizabeth's first born child. The last plague in Exodus was God's plan to kill the first born of every family in Egypt not protected by the blood of the lamb on the door lintel. Jews today still celebrate the Passover as one of their most Holy days. "First born" was the key. Smithson was not after President Bush, but the twins, George and Laura's only children. I'm bad about jumping to conclusions, so I wanted to be sure before I said anything. I had Sally go back through the file, and read me the last warning letter. It did not say that Smithson was going to kill the President, but that the plague would bring suffering.

I told the team my feeling about the twins, based on the "First born" plague, and they agreed it made sense. I told Bill Erickson that if his comment about the end of the plagues ended up helping us to catch the guy, then he had answered the challenge that I had given him about assisting the team. Even Sally smiled at my grudging admittance that Erickson might be earning his keep. I speed dialed Mark Sullivan. He was still wearing dual hats as head of the Secret Service, and the chair of the Smithson task force.

"Hi Mark. This is Bill Peterson."

Mark sounded harried. "Hi Bill. I heard you were off the team. Looking for a new job?"

I cut him off. "I don't have time for that right now. I'm with the team, and we think we've figured out what Smithson is doing. It looks like

193

he might be after the twins, Barbara and Jenna. Where are they?"

Bill said, "They went down to Austin this morning with their grandfather to see the Texas/Texas A&M football game. They are sitting in Red McComb's private box at the stadium, with 4 agents there to protect them."

I told him about our suspicions, and he agreed to try and get the former president and the girls to leave the game, to get his guys to do a good search of the private box, and a general search of the stadium. He said the Austin Secret Service people had access to the Austin Police Department's dogs, and that they had several dogs that could sniff for bombs. He said he would look into the itinerary for the twins for the rest of the weekend, but that he couldn't force them to do anything - that they had the authority to tell the Secret Service no, whenever they wanted to do their own thing.

I pulled out my government credit card, and called our waitress over. I told her, "Put everybody's bill on this - we have to go now." Erickson left the tip on the table, in cash, just to help get us out of there.

I told everyone to saddle up - we were headed for Austin as fast as we could get there. Ten minutes later we had 3 cars of agents headed south. The game was due to start at 11:00 AM Central time, the first in a series of games that would last all day on Friday. We were close to 90 miles away, and we would be fighting late arriving game traffic all the way into town. I called Sullivan back, and had him arrange a police escort for us from the Texas Department of Public Safety. Even with that, I was estimating an arrival of around 10:45 at the stadium - not much time to locate our suspect, and defuse any plans he had made for the twins. I asked Mark to double check every item of food and every bottle of drinks in that luxury suite, or anything coming into the suite today.

I didn't know for sure that he had planned anything for the stadium, but it seemed like the most likely scenario. Somehow he had found out that the twins were going to attend the game, and he was going to be there, too - or at least leave one of his calling cards there. We didn't want to have to evacuate the stadium, which would cause a major panic, or delay the start of the game, if at all possible. We didn't want to let Smithson know we were on to him, so that if he did plan to be there we could have a decent chance of grabbing him. In one sense we were using the 85,000 people attending the game as bait - but it was still our best chance, and we didn't want to miss the opportunity.

I had Sally and the reporter in the car with me as we drove south on I-35. I had each of them call one of the other cars, and put their cell phones on speaker phone, so that everyone could hear me.

"OK, this is the plan. We don't want to look like FBI agents in the stadium, so along with the

Secret Service people we will wear Aramark concession shirts and aprons, so that we look like soda or popcorn vendors in the stands. We will have copies of Smithson's picture waiting on us when we arrive, so that everyone can carry a copy. Be prepared for him to be in another disguise. My guess is that he could look like an ABC cameraman, a male cheerleader, which in the Aggie's case means that he will look like a milkman in a white uniform. He could look like a Texas Cowboy, or else one of those dedicated fans that paint their entire bodies in their school colors. He might even use the same concession shirt we are going to wear. The Texas cannon, "Old Smokey," is supposed to be loaded with blanks. Maybe he is going to try and get a live shell into that gun, and shoot it at McComb's box. You have to identify his face, and remember that he sometimes dresses like a girl. Don't let any disguise distract you."

I told the team, "We're going to divide up the seating sections when we get to the stadium, and we will check out every single person, row by row, in each section until we find this guy. I know in my gut that he will be here, and this will be our best chance to grab him. He may be armed, he may be prepared to be a suicide bomber, or something we haven't even considered. I don't think he is coming there just to wave at the Bush girls and then meekly surrender. We have to be prepared for anything. Wear your weapons out of sight, but where you can get to them quickly. The

Secret Service is giving us sets of their communication system earphones with built-in mikes so that we will be able to communicate with each other. Stay off the channel unless you spot the guy. And don't try and take him alone. Wait for backup if at all possible. We don't want to give him a chance to kill himself in a big fireball, and take a bunch of football fans with him."

Sally asked if she should call Tom Lawrence, and let him know what we suspected, and what we were doing to counteract the possible threat.

I may not officially be the team leader, but I made a command decision. "I say no. I'm afraid that he will think I am stepping on his toes, and call this off. I don't want to give him the chance to second guess us until this is over. I will take full responsibility for that decision, and tell him and the Director that I told you not to call him."

Mark Sullivan called me back, and gave me bad news. "The twins say this is a big game, for the Big XII South Division Championship, and unless you have some proof this guy is here, they don't want to leave. They are not sure they buy your theory that Smithson is after them instead of their father, and we can't make them stay in Crawford. They do promise to stay in the back of the luxury box, so that they can't be seen from the rest of the stands. They are going to a Kappa Alpha Theta Sorority party after the game, and they say the odds are just as good that he might try for them there." Mark added, "I'm open to

197

suggestions, but unless you can give me something else, I can't make them leave. Get me solid evidence to make it clear that Smithson is around here somewhere, and I will get that info to Snowstorm. He can still make his granddaughters do what needs to be done." Snowstorm is the Secret Service's code name for Bush 41.

I told Mark I would get back to him, and passed this complication on to the rest of the team. I had spent many a happy Saturday afternoon in Texas' Memorial Stadium, watching the Longhorns win. Now all I could see in my mind was the stadium, and 85,000 people, disappearing in a mushroom cloud.

Darrell K. Royal Texas Memorial Stadium
Austin, TX
10:34 AM Friday, November 25, 2006

We're here, and a few minutes earlier than I expected. The police escort down Interstate 35 helped. We're all getting dressed in our concessionaire shirts and hats. Guns are hidden, either under aprons, under the shirt in the back, or ankle holsters. Between the available Secret Service agents and my FBI team, we have 22 people to cover the entire stadium. Not enough to quickly and thoroughly search every face in the stadium. We are distributing pictures to the Austin police helping at the stadium, so that they can look for this guy, too. There are 39 sections in the bottom deck, and 18 more in upper decks on both the east and west sides of the stadium. The north and south end zones have only one level, as UT hasn't built decks over the lower stands for the "bad" seats. There are also luxury boxes hanging under the upper decks on both sides, but those are my last priority, with the exceptions of McComb's box, and the boxes on each side of his. I'm also not sure that Smithson knows the girls will be in McComb's box, although his intelligence on where people will be has been very good in the past. Robert Gates, the ex-President of Texas A&M and Bush's nominee to replace Donald Rumsfeld as Secretary of Defense, is also at the game in the visitor's box, and President Bush 41 and Gates are good friends. There is a chance that Smithson will think the girls are in that box with their Grandfather.

My guess is that he will be somewhere in the stands, or else on the concourse behind the luxury boxes, and will either do something to one of those boxes, create a diversion and try and gain access to the box himself, or do something to cause the box to be evacuated, and be waiting for the girls to come out the back door of the box. I'm hoping he doesn't have a bomb big enough to take out the entire stadium, or at least one side of the stands. We have agents with the girls, and people checking the door to McComb's luxury box closely. I don't think Smithson can gain access. Our best bet is to find him before he can pull anything.

Knowing how Smithson likes to pull stunts straight out of novels with stories on terrorists, I was assigning people to check all of the ABC trucks to make sure that none of them contained a bomb (one of Clancy's plots), when Sally saw all the camera monitors in the Producer's trailer, and came up with a great idea. She grabbed the ABC producer, and got him to give us two cameras for as long as we needed them. As I have learned from experience, she can be very persuasive when she wants to be! Her idea was to have those two cameras start at each end of the field, and pan every seat. With her computer background, she found a way to route those scans to our face recognition computer program in Washington, so that if the cameras and computers got a match, we would find Smithson that much faster. Everyone else headed for their assigned sections to start looking for our guy. My best guess is that he was going to be either directly across the stadium from McComb's box, in either the lower or the upper deck, or else back behind McComb's box. We concentrated most of our auxiliary resources in those areas. If I was wrong, the responsibility would be mine. My head was already on the chopping block, so what was one more mistake? A decision had to be made, and I made it - whether or not I was right would be determined by the outcome of our search, and whether or not we got to Smithson in time to save the Bush twins.

I got a call telling me that what the Austin police thought was Smithson's car had been located in the shopping center lot where people parked to catch the "Park 'n Ride" shuttle bus service to the game. A lot of people that did not have reserve parking around the stadium (which required that you donate big bucks to the Longhorn Foundation each year) rode the shuttle buses to and from the stadium for every game. That confirmed that he was probably here, but somehow I knew that already. He wouldn't miss the chance to show off in front of a national TV audience. I started to get Mark Sullivan to use that evidence to get the girls out of the stadium, but with the crowds already here I was afraid that was what Smithson wanted. I figured they were probably safer in their luxury suite than they would be fighting their way out against the current of people still swarming into the stadium. We told everyone through their earpiece communicators that we now knew that Smithson was in the area, in case anyone had previously had any doubts. Either we stopped him before he could act, or a lot of people could end up dead and injured.

Then Tom Lawrence called and interrupted me. His first comment was, "Just what the hell do you think you're doing? You don't run that team anymore. What makes you think Smithson is there?" Apparently when Sally set up the face recognition search program someone in Washington had called Lawrence to let him know what we were doing.

I said, "Mr. Lawrence, you've heard my theory about our perp following the Exodus scenario. In this case, I think he is trying to copy the 10th plague in Exodus, going after the first born, the Bush twins. I have been told that the Austin police have located a Honda like the one we were searching for in the game area, so we are even more convinced he is here somewhere."

Tom wasn't buying any of it. He told me, "This is just more of your conjecture, and you really don't have a single fact to hang your hat on. As soon as I can get hold of the team, I'm ordering them back to Crawford. That's where the real threat is - not in Austin. I'm ordering you to stand down - you have no authority in Austin, and I want you to leave immediately."

I had finally had enough from him. I told him, "Mr. Lawrence, will all due respect, you can stick your orders for me to stand down. I'm still an FBI agent, and I considered myself bound by my oath to defend the Constitution, and not bound by orders from someone who said to me, and I quote, 'You'll never be a team leader, and I'll never have you working for me again.' You are no longer my boss, you are dead wrong in this case, and I don't have time for your crap." I hung up on him, and went back to planning how to catch our guy. I knew I would be in trouble later for what I had done, but I had taken enough Bevo excreta from Lawrence, and I still felt that this opportunity was our best chance to catch Smithson.

My guess was that whatever he was planning would occur either late in the 1st Quarter, or early in the 2nd. He would want to make sure his intended victims were on the scene, so he would give them a chance to arrive, even if they were fashionably late. And he would also consider that young women are sometimes not the most ardent of football fans (although it has been my experience that a lot of Texas women are raised to love the sport), and the twins might be planning on leaving early, and possibly as early as halftime. After all, the Friday after Thanksgiving is the heaviest shopping day of the year, and the girls might prefer spending Daddy's (or their Grandfather's) money over watching Texas beat the Aggie plowboys back into fertilizer. So sometime in that time span, between the first and second quarters, I expected whatever was going to happen to start. But, I could be way off in my estimate of when he would strike. We needed to get to him first, and fast.

The concession vendor pattern was to come out of the ramp entrance, work the lower seats in each section, and then climb toward the top. You had to be in good shape to be a vendor here - the stadium had 60 rows in both the lower and upper decks, with 30 rows in the end zones, so the concession people working the stands did a lot of climbing during each game. We had decided to have our people pretending to sell programs. The thought process was that selling programs would mean fewer customers, since most people that wanted one would have already bought one on the way into the stadium, and that dropping the programs to pull a gun would be easier than dropping a tray of sodas, or a box carrying bags of popcorn. We told our people not to advertise - that they didn't have to shout "Programs!" as they walked and searched. If they had to make a sale, I told them to go ahead and make it - but to ignore requests for programs if they could, and not to actually try and make money. I told them I was not giving bonuses for who sold the most programs, but that I would give something to whoever identified our bad guy. They understood the role, and everyone headed to their assigned sections, with the exception of Sally. She stayed with the ABC people to help coordinate the face identification program. I headed for the sections directly across the stadium from McComb's box.

When I came out of the ramp entrance into the stadium itself, I stayed back in the shadows a little bit, and used a pair of binoculars to scan the luxury boxes across the field. I could see into McComb's box, but I couldn't see the twins. At least they were following their Secret Service agents' advice, and staying towards the back of the box. I walked down to the front row of my section, and started working my way back to the top. I hadn't realized how tough identifying anyone would be from this angle. A lot of people were wearing sunglasses, hiding their faces with scarves and hats, drinking from a stadium cup, using binoculars and cameras, or talking on a cell phone. And no one was sitting still - people were jumping up and down on almost every play, showing their emotions as the fortunes of their favorite team climbed to the highest heights, and dropped to the lowest lows. Since this was mostly a Texas crowd, especially in these good seats between the 40 yard lines, there were a lot of people in my sections standing and cheering. Texas was in a close game, and the fans wanted their team to murder A&M on the field. I just wanted to make sure that was the only murder committed here today. I wasn't having much luck finding our boy, but I still had nearly 50 rows to scan in just the bottom deck of the stadium.

As it turned out, I was dead wrong. OK, I was right about Smithson being in the stadium, but embarrassingly incorrect about WHERE he was in the stands. I thought he would be in the middle of the stands across from McComb's luxury box, where he would have a good view of what he was targeting. Instead, he was on the top row of the north end zone, almost exactly in the middle between the goalpost uprights, where the field goal kickers would try and aim. Sally's identification program found the guy after only about 10 minutes of checking faces, before I could even make it half way up the sections I was searching. It would have taken us hours, but the computers are much faster than the human eye.

Sally's voice sounded excited even through my earpiece, as she said, "We found him.

He's wearing face paint, a Texas baseball cap, and a big coat. I can't tell if he is armed or not because of the coat. He could even have explosives under that jacket."

We didn't want to alarm the guy, and get him to prematurely set off whatever he had planned, so we decided to try and approach him with just a couple of people - one on each aisle on each side of his section.

We put a Secret Service sharpshooter on top of the Longhorn's practice facility just past the south end zone, with a clear shot at Smithson if it looked like he was going to pull a weapon. It would be a tough shot, with people jumping up and down in the stands in front of our guy, but the Secret Service people are good at what they do, too. I hoped to take him alive if at all possible. I went up the west stairway, and Sally took the east one, so that we were on each side of the section where he was sitting. I thought she deserved a chance at the collar, since it was her idea that gave us the chance us to find the guy. Sally and I were still dressed in concessionaire outfits, so hopefully we would not be obvious to Smithson until we could get close enough to try and grab him. Getting to the top of the stadium was not that big a problem - lots of people liked the high seats, and climbed all the way up to get that perspective of the game and the field. What would be dangerous would be our attempt to work our way down the seating aisle toward our guy. Every row of bleachers was full, and he had to notice us sooner or later, but we were going to try and keep our approach as unobtrusive as possible. If that was even possible with someone as paranoid as Smithson. I was just hoping we weren't all going to disappear in a big fireball.

Sally and I made it to the top of the stairs without any problems, taking our time. It was now about 5 minutes into the second quarter of the game, so I knew we were probably getting short on time - Smithson could be making his play at any time. Sally and I glanced at each other, and we both nodded. We started inching our way into Smithson's aisle, working toward him from both sides. Even the end zone stands were full, so it was tough getting around people.

Suddenly my communicator went off in my ear. "Be careful! He just pulled a box with switches on it out of his coat pocket - something's going down! Sally and I both reached for our weapons.

The guy next to where I was standing saw my pistol, and started screaming, "Gun! Gun! He's got a gun!"

People started bailing out of the way, and suddenly there was no one between me and our perp. But I could also hear a strange whine coming from off to my left, out past the edge of the stands - and then the biggest model plane I had ever seen flew almost directly over Sally's head, heading out over the stands and the field. Everybody on that side of Smithson ducked, including Sally, and I flinched. It was an involuntary reaction to the sudden appearance of the plane, and I couldn't resist being startled, too.

Unfortunately, Smithson knew what was coming, and used the distraction to his advantage. With everybody's eyes drawn to the plane, he tossed what had to be the plane's controller at me. And as I automatically tried to catch the remote control, Smithson leaped over the side of the stadium! I jumped for him, trying to grab him, but I was still too far away from him and missed - and only then did I see the rope that he had tied to the rail behind where he had been sitting. He was sliding down the rope so fast that I hoped he would break a leg when he hit the bottom - but he slowed himself just in time, jumped the rest of the way to the ground, and looked back up at me. There were a few people down on the ground around him giving him strange looks, but no cops. Why is there never a cop around when you need one? I thought for a second about trying to shoot him as he scooted down the rope, but there were too many people on the ground in the area under the stadium wall and around the north gate.

He cupped his mouth with his hands and shouted up at me, "Fly good - there's one hell of a bomb in that plane!"

He gave me a little two-fingered salute, turned, and sprinted for the open gate. We didn't have anyone on the ground to stop him. And I realized I had a bigger problem. I was holding the controls for a flying bomb in my hand, and I didn't know squat about how to fly a model plane.

But then I knew that I did. The switches were labeled on the front of the radio controller: throttle, ailerons, and rudder. That was simpler than flying the Cessna I had flown in Wisconsin! The plane, because everything had automatically set back to neutral when Smithson released the controls, was flying nice and level down the middle of the field toward the south end zone. The teams had stopped playing, and without anyone requesting an official break each team (and the referees) had retired to the sidelines. Everyone was watching the plane. I knew I didn't want to crash the plane in the stadium, and I knew that it probably didn't have enough fuel in it to fly long enough for us to evacuate the entire place - so I had to find another place to set it down. I thought about the practice field out past the south end zone, but there were people up there, too, and I didn't know the range of the controller. I tried a gentle turn with the controller, and the plane headed for the east stands. People on that side of the stadium started screaming. Another quarter turn, and it was flying back toward us in the north end zone stands. Our end of the field was pretty empty by this time, because of the altercation with Smithson, but I didn't even want to think about bringing the plane in where I was standing. I wanted it out of the stadium, so I increased the power a little, using the throttle control, to help the plane climb. I flew it over the flagpoles behind me and out of the stands. I wasn't sure how far the range was on the remote, so I didn't want to get the plane too far away from me. I could just see it getting out of range, and flying into the hospital just north of campus. I found a combination of settings that allowed the plane to make lazy circles just north of the stadium, a couple of hundred feet off the ground. For some reason I flashed back to that series of Airplane! movies that came out back in the '80's - here I was trying to fly something I really didn't know anything about, with very dangerous consequences if I failed.

Sally was standing beside me, and trying to make sense out of all the noise coming through our earpieces. She finally told everyone to shut up, because I was busy.

She sent people looking for Smithson, and then asked me, "What do you need?"

I said, "A place to set this down, with no people around, and secure enough so that if there is a bomb on the plane, and it explodes, no one will get hurt."

All I could see from the stands were the tops of big buildings - the Fine Arts building, the edge of the Texas Ex Student Center back to the west, the Band Hall across the street from the stadium, the LBJ Library with the big fountain out front another block to the north from the stadium, the Performing Arts Center, and so on. The stadium is built on the Northeast corner of the campus, so there are not a lot of University buildings past where I was standing. I knew immediately that the Ex-Student Center was out. It would already be full of half-drunk fans, watching the game there instead of coming into the stadium. The roof tops of the other buildings didn't seem flat enough or big enough to use as a runway for the plane. This thing was huge. Silver in color, it looked like it had a wingspan about 6 or 8 ft. long, and the entire model looked big enough to take small children for rides. Speaking of being taken for a ride, was there really a bomb in the plane? I thought there probably was, but there was no way to be sure - it might have been just another distraction by Smithson, set up to keep us occupied while he got away.

I took another look around, and made my decision.

"Sally, get them to open both of the front double doors to the band hall, where the band comes marching out before the game. Make sure the building is evacuated. I'm going to try and fly the plane into that building."

She got on the mike, and started issuing orders. It was probably only 5 or 6 minutes later when she told me everything was ready, but it seemed like it had been a couple of hours. She said the building had been evacuated, and that the doors were propped open. The band hall was right across the street from where I was standing at the top of the stands, and I could see the entranceway pretty well. I took the plane out of its circle, lined it up with the doors to the band hall,

211

and started a glide down toward the ground. My idea was to land the plane just as it entered the building. I had never been in the band hall, but I was thinking that there should be a lot of open space inside the building, since that is where the band members lined up prior to marching over to the stadium for each game. I decided I had better check to make sure, and pulled the plane up again, back into a circle.

I told Sally, "Get someone down there to tell me how much open space there is inside those doors."

She checked, and came back a couple of minutes later to tell me that it was open all the way to the back of the building, a space of about two hundred feet. She said there was nothing in that room but a few band instruments. I brought the plane back down again, lining it up with the doors. I thought about having someone try and shut the doors after the plane landed, but decided that there was too much of a chance of an immediate explosion, and that anyone standing in the doorway would get the full force of the blast. I told Sally to keep everyone away from the doorway, and to make sure the street was empty between the building and the stadium. I was afraid that when the plane went inside the building I would lose all control, and that I wouldn't be able to cut the throttle on the plane, bringing it to a stop. For a moment, it crossed my mind that I could put the plane back in a circle, shimmy down the rope that Smithson had used, and control the plane better from the ground. But I was also worried about all the metal in the fencing around the stadium, the overhang of the stands, and the big ornamental gateway at the north end of the stadium grounds. If anything interfered with the plane's controls, it could end up anywhere, with major damages and injuries resulting.

I had to live with the decision I had already made. I slowed the plane, trying to get a feel for how slow it could fly without stalling. I didn't want to land it any faster than I had to, but at the same time I wanted it flying all the way to the entrance to the band hall without diving straight into the ground. I decided that too much speed was better than too little, so I brought it in a little hot. The landing was actually pretty good. I had the nose up, and the plane not more than six inches off the ground, as it flew into the double door opening of the building. I immediately chopped the throttle back to zero, but I didn't know if that had caused the plane to slow, or if it was continuing on its way with the last instructions received before flying through the doors. It didn't take but a few seconds to find out. Suddenly there was a huge explosion, blowing out all the windows in the building, and an expanding fireball came blasting back out the double door entry. About half of the roof collapsed, and immediately flames could be seen licking at the edges of the remaining roofline. I didn't know how much Semtex the guy had loaded into the plane, but I was glad that the plane had not been flown into McComb's luxury box! I nearly collapsed, and had to grab the edge of the seat behind me for support.

Sally told me to sit down for a minute. She said, "There is nothing else you can do right now, and you need a break after that stunt. You're a hero for saving all of the people in here."

All I could say was, "Well, I'm not sure the band will agree with that. I ruined their building. I can already see the homework excuses they will be using next week."

We both started laughing hysterically.

It took a while to get things organized after that. The remainder of the game was postponed, to be continued tomorrow, Saturday, November 26th. They had to get the game finished quickly, because if Texas won they would have to play in the Big XII championship game in Kansas City on Saturday, December 3rd. Postponing the championship game would make it tough on the football players, because all of the universities that might play in that game would be getting into finals in December. ABC said they would work out the game coverage for Saturday, even if Texas was the only area in the country to get the rest of the game. I figured that after today, anything they broadcast from Austin would probably get great ratings, but I didn't want to tell them how to run their business.

People were allowed to leave the stadium, but it took hours to clear the area. The normal Park 'n Ride passenger pickup point had been at the northwest corner of the stadium, but that was still too close to the band hall, so the Austin police had to move that bus pickup site back to the south end of the sports complex. That took extra time, along with getting people that had parked in the parking garages further north on campus maneuvered around the bomb scene and back to their cars. Traffic was a nightmare. The fire department even had trouble getting their equipment on scene to fight the fire.

We also had all sorts of people flying in to the Austin airport, out at the old Bergstrom Air Force Base location east of town. Back when Bergstrom was a Strategic Air Command Base, full of B-52s and H-bombs, the huge gas tank near the main gate had the SAC motto painted on it - "Peace is our Profession." I had always wanted the FBI to adopt that. I kind of like to think that "Peace" is what we are striving for, too. Flying in to the scene of this latest attempted attack were bomb experts, more agents to assist in the search for Smithson, and my ex-boss, Tom Lawrence. I wasn't too sure where I stood with the Bureau, but I knew exactly where I stood with Tom. He told me to stay on the scene until he arrived, even if that meant I had to stay there all night.

He said, "I understand that you didn't cover every possible exit, and so I'm blaming you for letting this guy escape again. I plan on bringing you up on charges for dereliction of duty. If you had stayed out of things, like you were supposed to, we might have him in jail right now."

Just what I needed to hear. He didn't even mention my insubordination, but I knew that he had probably already discussed that with the Director, and I was sure that he had charges pending on what I had said to him, too. I was sure that I already had an appointment pending with the FBI's Office of Professional Responsibility. The fact that without my involvement the Bush twins might be dead right now was something Lawrence probably hadn't even considered. It is just like him to rush in after things are over, and try to Monday morning quarterback. Hindsight is always 20/20. Of course I should have had someone on the ground underneath where Smithson was sitting. But who expected him to try and escape in that direction? It was my fault, and I knew I was wrong. In the heat of the moment, I had failed to cover that possible escape path. But I had done a few things right, and I didn't want to have to listen to Lawrence tell me how we should have discovered the plan earlier, taken more time to develop a strategy to stop Smithson, found the bomb before the game, never let him get to his seat, and so on - all the things that could have been done if we had used what few brains we apparently did have (according to Lawrence). I guess we should have tried a crystal ball for guidance, too. I could almost write out his chewing I was going to get, he was so predictable. But I would rather he jump on me, and leave the rest of the team alone. If I can protect them from his wrath, my taking the punishment will be worth it.

James Smith
Journal Entry
Saturday, November 25, 2006

Yesterday was frustrating as all get out. I'm so mad I could turn loose the rest of my left-over bugs on the whole state of Texas, especially if that would help get rid of any of the Bush family - and I still have some samples hidden in different places around the country. I was less than three minutes from success with my mini version of 9/11, and would have taken out the Bush first born, just like the plague in the Bible, when that damn lucky FBI agent Peterson had to barge in. I recognized him the minute I heard someone yell "Gun!" and I looked down the bleacher row. His picture has been in the paper, too - not just mine. I started to just plow the plane into the middle of the field, or into the stands to create a diversion - but I guessed that they would shoot me if I did that. So I bailed. I told you my dad and his buddies at Bragg had taught me to always have a backup escape plan! I didn't think I would need the rope. I had planned on fleeing the stadium with the rest of the fans after the explosion in the luxury box, just another person trying to get away from the blast and fire. But after they found me, and I'll have to figure out how they did that, my best bet was to just get away, to live to fight another day. After I got out of the stadium, I hotwired a car, recovered my backpack, drove south to San Marcos, stole another car there, and drove it to San Antonio (I didn't think that the FBI would guess that I would head south instead of north.) I dumped the 2nd stolen car there, took a bus ride to Houston, and then another bus from there to Dallas. I got to Dallas early this morning. I bought another old raggedy used car in South Oak Cliff, from a place that took cash and didn't ask too many questions. I'm now in a motel in Waxahachie, a town south of Dallas, but far enough north of Waco that I don't think the Secret Service or the FBI would be checking motels for my smiling face. I'm down to my last "unknown" name on a credit card, other than James Smith, so whatever I do I have to be careful with this identity. This may be my last chance to take action before I have to flee the country.

I'm back in my "Lisa" disguise. Peterson got too good a look at me in the stands before I jumped the railing, and I don't want to be recognized. I don't think people will be looking for a woman. My credit card just has initials on it, so the name could be a woman's just as easily as it could belong to a man. If I ever get to the point where I have another girlfriend, or even possibly get married, I swear I will never complain about how long it takes my lady to put on her makeup. You have to do it slowly to do it right, and it can take forever - as I've discovered trying to make

218

myself look a little more like a female. I have to be careful using public restrooms, reminding myself which door to go in, but other than that I think I can pull this off without too many problems. I look a little like Dustin Hoffman did in "Tootsie." I'm a brunette this time around.

As for Peterson, I've developed a real hatred for the guy. First he dissed me when I wrote him my letter, and he has been a thorn in my side all through this campaign. There is no doubt in my mind that without his involvement on Friday I would have succeeded in killing the President's daughters. There was a long article about Peterson in the Dallas Morning News this morning, by that reporter Erickson that is working with the FBI, going on and on about how Peterson was so brilliant, how he saved 85,000 people, including the Bush girls and their grandfather, and how Peterson should be given a medal for his heroism. The article discussed how Peterson had been in Waco, and made the connection that I was after the Bush twins instead of George W from the pastor's comments in a sermon at the First Baptist Church. I may just have to attend services there tomorrow, to see if our hero is still attending. I think he is deserving of some of my toys, even if he doesn't have anything to do with our troops in Iraq - other than being the devil that is keeping me from completing my God-appointed mission. I guess I need to go buy Lisa a Sunday dress. See you in church, y'all!

219

Chapter 9

Bill Peterson
Waco, Texas
9:33 AM Sunday, November 26, 2006

The bad news is that we missed Smithson. Somehow he again found a way to elude our nets. We can't be far behind him, but I have to admit this guy is good. You almost have to admire someone that can keep out of our clutches for this length of time. The good news is that I am back in charge of my team. Apparently Mark Sullivan decided that the Secret Service needed to recognize what I had done to save the Bush girls, and the rest of the 85,000 people in the stands at the football game, so he called Director Mueller and told him what had really happened. By the time Lawrence got to Austin, he was the one that had been reassigned, and I was back in charge.

I called Mark, to tell him how much I appreciated what he had done, and his only response was, "Pay me back by finding this guy, and do it fast."

My team is back in the Waco area, because we don't think Smithson is going to give up.

I was embarrassed by the article that appeared in the paper this morning. The Waco paper picked up the Saturday article from the Washington Post because of the local connection to the church, so the few people that know me here in town have been calling all morning, congratulating me. I don't think congratulations are in order just yet, because our perp is still out there, and until we shut him down permanently there is still a chance that he could succeed in killing someone else.

Church this morning should be interesting. I wonder what Dr. Walker will have to say, if anything, about what happened? Julie is not real thrilled that I am back "officially" looking for our bad guy. She knows that I am not only ambitious, but that I am obsessed with finding this guy and putting him down because of what he did to our family. She is a better Christian than I am. She can forgive, and let God do the judging. I'm ready to be judge, juror, and hangman.

James Smith
Journal Entry
Sunday, November 26, 2006

I almost got up from the church service this morning and walked out. I would have done it if it wouldn't have brought too much attention. The church pastor actually had the FBI guy stand up, and the entire church then stood up and applauded him. I couldn't stand it! What I'm doing is the Lord's work, and this idiot Peterson keeps trying to stop that. Since he doesn't seem to grasp that truth, I guess I'll have to get him out of the way. Sometimes you have to fight minor

221

devils before you can get to the big ones. If Peterson is standing between me and the Bush family, if he is the one keeping me from getting to Crawford, then he will have to go.

I followed Peterson and his wife, and I guess his Mother-in-Law (he wasn't listed in the phone book, so I guess the phone is in the Mother-in-Law's name), after they left church. They went out to eat, and then back to a house on the northwest side of town, right on the river. I started to go into the restaurant after them, but I thought that might be tempting fate a little too much. I sat in the car in a parking lot of another restaurant across the street until they paid for their lunch and left. I went hungry for an extra couple of hours, and I'm adding that to Peterson's tally sheet of sins, too. The sermon this morning was on turning the other cheek. Hah! "Vengeance is mine, sayeth the Lord," is quoted in both the Books of Hebrews, and in Paul's Letter to the Romans. But sometimes the Lord uses people as his sword for obtaining that vengeance. I am that sword, and I will be that sword until this task is done.

I spent all afternoon thinking about the best way to take care of Peterson. That home on the river kept coming back to my thoughts. I haven't used water itself as a plague, other than putting a few flu bugs in the water in D.C. It doesn't take much water to make a flood, or much of a flood to do major damage or to cause major injuries - including drownings. I still have plenty of

Semtex. I've still got my trusty backpack, because I had hidden it in Austin before I left for the stadium. Even though I didn't like carrying all of that explosive material around with me as I bounced around southeast Texas, I didn't have a choice if I wanted to have the stuff readily available. If I could figure out a way to get their house into the river, or get the river into their house, it could get interesting for the Petersons.

The Brazos River is dammed not too far upstream from the Peterson's place, so there is not normally much of a flow going by their neighborhood. Maybe I will have to help nature again, to help me get to that final goal. Waco Lake holds over 500,000 acre feet of water behind an earthen dam that sits 148 feet above the streambed. If I could send that much water down on the Peterson family home, all those swimming lessons I'm sure Bill Peterson took as a kid wouldn't do him much good.

God used a flood coming down on the Pharaoh's army, as they tried to cross the Nile chasing after the Hebrews escaping from slavery, as a final punishment on Egypt. If that was good enough for the army of Egypt, then it ought to be good enough for a lowly FBI agent. Isn't it amazing how much strategy can be gained from one Book in the Bible? Exodus was a well-planned campaign, just like mine. Of course, when God brings the plagues directly, the odds of survival are much lower than when they have to go through His humble servant, yours' truly. But I do what I can. So why wait? I'm already in town. So come on in, the water's fine!

Bill Peterson
Waco, Texas
7:55 PM Sunday, November 26, 2006

I felt like I had eyes watching me all morning in church. It wasn't a very comfortable feeling. I had a feeling that I would be recognized some way in church this morning, especially after telling Erickson about how the sermon last Sunday helped me to figure out what Smithson was going to attempt. I expected some crack about how "at least one person was listening last Sunday" or else, "God works in mysterious ways." But I wasn't expecting to be made to stand, and to get a long round of applause and a standing ovation from what is usually a pretty mild bunch of parishioners. I had played baseball at Texas, a great college baseball program, for UT coach Cliff Gustafson in front of 5,000 screaming fans at Disch-Falk Field, and even played at the College World Series in Omaha in front of nearly 15,000 people. But this ovation in church was the first time I was ever embarrassed to hear people clapping for me. Both Julie and her Mom told me they were proud of me - and I think that's the first compliment I've ever gotten from Margaret.

The funny thing is that I still had a nagging feeling like I had eyes on me after we left the church. I didn't think anyone in the restaurant we

224

visited for lunch had been at the same church service, but Waco is a pretty small town, so I guess it was possible. I don't like feeling uncomfortable, thinking that someone is watching me. I will never be cut out for the limelight. I guess stars in Hollywood get that paranoia feeling all the time. I wonder if they ever get used to it, or learn to ignore the stares?

I just couldn't stop thinking about Smithson, even during my lunch conversation with Julie and Margaret. I had no clue what he was going to try next, or how we were going to stop him - if we could stop him. As many tricks as he has pulled out of his bag, I wouldn't put anything past him at this point - whether or not it was something out of the Bible.

I'm meeting with my team at Margaret's house at 8:00 this evening, in just a few minutes. She was kind enough to offer to let everyone come here, instead of us meeting in some motel room. Of course, that meant that we had to vacuum the whole house, clean the bathrooms, sweep the front porch and sidewalk, and make the place look like a model home up for sale - Margaret wasn't about to have company without her house ready to shine!

We have got to come up with a strategy that will save the President and his family. If Smithson was to kill George Bush, the entire country might end up in a Constitutional crisis. The President has not yet named a replacement for the late Vice President, so if the President was to be killed, the Speaker of the House would assume the mantle of power as President - not something that would sit well with at least half of the country.

That is especially true right now, because there will be a new Speaker taking office in January, when the new election results tilt the balance of power to the Democrats. How to handle that problem is way above my pay grade. All I want to do is catch an uncommon criminal that is invading my dreams every night. I'm fresh out of ideas. I'm hoping the team can come through with something that will lead us to this guy, and quickly. I have a feeling that his backup plan to his backup plan will not take long to be put into action - and we can't afford to give him that chance.

Waco, Texas
8:15 PM Sunday, November 26, 2006

We had just settled down to a brainstorming session when Julie and Margaret brought in coffee and some of Margaret's famous Strawberry Angel Food Cake, with melted chocolate dribbled over the cake slices and fresh strawberries, instead of the usual whipped cream you get with strawberry shortcake. We had to take a quick break to eat - the stuff is better while the chocolate is still warm from melting. Julie asked how things were going.

I said, "Not very well. We have no clue what he will pull next."

She asked, "Well, what plagues has he not yet tried?"

Sally spoke up. "We still have some form of lice, flies, and locusts to go. I guess lice could represent some other type of disease, but I don't see how flies or locusts could be used to do real damage."

Margaret chimed in with her genteel southern drawl. "Y'all do know there is one more stunt God and Moses pulled in that story - the parting of the waters of the Nile, and the resulting flood that wiped out the Egyptian army."

We all looked at each other - we had not even thought about a flood.

"Margaret," I asked, trying to act calmer than I felt, "Do you have a Texas map we could borrow?"

She went to find one. The entire room was quiet, with everyone trying to reconstruct in their heads the watershed for the Crawford area. Margaret walked back in with a folded map, and we pressed it flat on the dining room table.

The good news is that it was pretty obvious there wasn't any way to flood the President's ranch. There were some creeks in the area that might flood naturally after some heavy rains, but nothing that would damage the President's home or any of the other buildings on his property. We all gave a big sigh of relief, especially knowing that we had not even considered the possibility until Margaret had brought it up.

Bill Erickson swallowed another bite of cake, and said, "I hate to bring up this point, but this house is sitting right on a river bank. The map does show a long dam upstream. Is there any chance that Smithson might decide to go after you, especially since it was you that stopped his last attack?"

We all looked at each other again, and then back at the map. It was just as obvious that a breach of the Waco Lake dam would put Margaret's house under about 20 tons of water within minutes.

I said, "I don't think he would come after me personally, but I did feel earlier today like someone was watching me."

This was a tough decision. Did I want to commit the team and other outside resources on a long shot, just on the gut feeling that Smithson might want to come after me, too?

For some reason, I flashed back to my Little League baseball days. I came in as a relief pitcher in the 9th inning of a game, 2 outs, with a runner on third base. The third base coach thought I was ignoring the runner on third, when in fact I could see him in my peripheral vision. I had always had a wide field of vision, and I could see him taking his lead from third out of the corner of my eye, without me actually having to stop my windup and look at the runner.

The third base coach told the runner to try and steal home since I was apparently ignoring the runner and his ever widening lead off the base. I think the runner was either confused or scared, because he hesitated. He didn't start toward home plate until I was well into my windup. I saw the runner going, and I went ahead and threw home. The runner was out by about ten feet after the tag by the catcher, ending the ball game.

After the game, our coach sat us all down in the outfield and talked to the team. "What you saw tonight is what happens when you hesitate. Either you go or you don't go, but you have to decide, and then stick with your decision. To hesitate will cost you every time."

That advice had stuck with me ever since I heard that speech. And after hearing that I've never had a problem making a decision, right or wrong. I've always been the full-speed ahead type - "either lead, follow, or get out of the way."

So I didn't hesitate when I made this decision. I told the team, "There is a chance he may come after me. And right now, we don't have any other leads to pursue. It wouldn't hurt to check out the dam, just in case there is a way he could use that as a way to attack me."

We dumped our planned meeting agenda, and started using our online resources to see what we could find about the local lake and the dam. Sally pulled up a bird's eye view of the dam and lake on her laptop, and turned the screen so

229

that we could all see the picture. The dam itself was massive. It was a wide earthen dam, over two miles long, with enough packed soil in it to keep even the most determined bomber from being able to breach the dam - with one exception. The area around the spillway looked like it might be vulnerable. The spillway, a little over 500 ft. long, was built from reinforced concrete. It was pretty wide on the downstream side, to help hold back the lake, but the outlet area was described on the lake's Internet home page as having a "20-foot diameter conduit passing under the dam."

Someone with enough Semtex could breach the dam at the conduit location, and the power of the water itself would tear the rest of the spillway to pieces. Half of Waco and Baylor could be flooded as a result. For all I knew half of Texas A&M would disappear, too, and that campus was another 80 miles downstream. There was no question that if the dam was to go, Margaret's house would collapse under a wall of water. Was this guy mad enough at me to come after me in a personal vendetta? There was no way of telling - but it was the best (and only) possibility we had at the moment, so it was worth investigating.

I told Margaret and Julie that it might be better if they left and stayed with Margaret's sister, Martha, in Dallas for a few days. "I don't want to alarm you, but I don't want anything to happen to either of you." They went to pack. I heard sobs from our bedroom, so I excused myself from the group, went to join Julie, and shut the door. She was in tears. I put my arms around her, but it was obvious she was upset about having to leave, and us be separated one more time. "Why can't this guy leave us alone?" Julie sputtered between sobs. "And I'm worried about you, and what might happen to you if you go after Smithson." I told her that I would be careful, and that we would have a lot of backup if we managed to figure out where Smithson was and what his plans were. "I don't want you to have to leave, but I think it is probably for the best." I told her. "Hopefully this will not be for long, and maybe we can get lucky this time and grab him. He is bound to make a mistake sooner or later." Julie didn't seem mollified, but she did go back to packing. I hugged her again, and went back out to join the rest of the team.

I had Sally call her old boyfriend Wally, because he worked for the Corps of Engineers. The U.S. Army Corps of Engineers was the organization that controlled the dam, the lake, and all the parks dotting the lakeshore. We worked our way up the Corps' food chain until we found someone that could make decisions, Major General Don T. Riley, the Director of Civil Works. General Riley didn't understand why we would be calling him at home on a Sunday evening, until we explained our suspicions about Smithson and the Corps' dam in Waco. I asked if the General could give us a local contact, so that we could have someone show us the dam area. I told him I realized that it was already dark, but that if Smithson was involved in this, then time was of the essence. That got his attention, and he had people on the way to meet us within a few minutes. As soon as I heard back from him that his people were on the way to meet us, we piled into a couple of cars again, and headed for the dam. It was too early to start notifying people like the Waco police EOD team, based strictly on our suspicions, but I had Andy start making contingency notification plans and phone lists, just in case we found something. Julie and her mom left when we did, heading for Dallas. I hated to see them go. I almost got in the car with them, just to make sure they would be safe on the trip.

It wasn't far up Lakeshore Drive to the dam. The entrance was fenced and the gate was shut and locked, but the Corps of Engineers Lieutenant that met us there had a key to the gate. We took his pickup, piled everybody in the front and back, and drove out onto the road that ran along the top of the dam. The far end was the area that we were interested in, and it took us about 10 minutes to make it in the dark to the spillway area. We couldn't see much, even with our flashlights and the existing lights on the dam, but it was obviously a place fairly easy to get to, and fairly easy to breach with enough explosives. We didn't know how much Semtex and dynamite, if any, that Smithson had left. But if he had enough, this section of the dam could be brought down.

The approach we had made, down the length of the dam, did not seem practical. There were three other ways to get to the spillway - from the water (there was a marina not far from the dam), from the marshy old riverbed and overflow area downstream from the dam, and from the Waco airport. The airport property adjoined the lake property, and the airport perimeter road was the only access to the dam road from the northwest end of the dam.

The simplest solution, if someone wanted to get to the spillway area, was through the marshy area downstream from the dam. There was an unofficial experimental outdoor environmental lab area just below the spillway, where a couple of nutria had built a small dam across the down flow stream from the lake, making a small, shallow pond. That pond and the surrounding area was being studied for local wildlife, and also as a stop along the flyway to Mexico for birds migrating from the Midwest and Canada. It wouldn't be much of a hike from the road leading to the pond site to make it to the dam through that area.

The airport route would be a little tougher, but could be done - the Waco airport site was not exactly a bastion of security, even with a sitting President living just a few miles southeast of town. Usually Air Force One flew into Fort Hood, the huge army base further south, close to

Killeen, and then the President and his family would be helicoptered to his ranch. A few reporters flew in and out of Waco, but the official Presidential party didn't come through here. So the Waco airport was only a small feeder airport for the Dallas/Fort Worth monster hub on the northwest side of Dallas, and for Houston Intercontinental, and security wasn't any different from any other small airport. I had flown into Waco before, and I could have easily have made it across the tarmac to the dam road.

To really be efficient, Smithson would have to waterproof his explosives, and dive on the lake side of the spillway to find the critical spot to place his explosives, at the entrance to the conduit under the spillway. That would be extremely dangerous, because you could get sucked into that conduit. It was possible to "fish" for the opening, by putting the explosives on a fishing line, and moving up and down the spillway until you felt the current swinging the explosives into the right place. Of course, at that point, you either had to go ahead and set them off, with you sitting on top of them in a boat, or weigh them down enough to settle on the bottom at the entrance to the conduit, with a timer already set for the designated blast time. Possible, but not too probable.

Now that we had reconnoitered the area, we had to determine how best to protect the dam, considering that we didn't know if it could even be considered a viable threat. Putting a police car on the road on the southeast end of the dam would stop anyone from coming in the way we did, but none of us thought our perp would come that way, anyway. Much more likely were the other three approaches, and we started making plans to cover all three possibilities. What we came up with was a set of stealthy stakeouts. We wanted Smithson to step into our trap. We didn't want to scare him off - we wanted him in handcuffs and shackles. I didn't mention that I wouldn't mind too much if he ended up dead, either. Instead of a police car on the southeast access road, we came up with a plan to place someone just out of sight of the road, where they could see if anyone tried to come in from that direction.

We put people in place for Sunday night, in shifts, covering both the marsh and the airport approaches. We got everyone the heaviest coats we could find, because it was going to be cold out there at night. We just about bought out the local Wal-Mart's supply of hats, gloves, and hand warmers. We didn't want any agents dying of pneumonia! We arranged for an unmarked Texas Parks and Wildlife boat to "fish" in the area of the dam all night long, with some of our agents rotating shifts on board the boat, to make sure Smithson didn't try to place the explosives before daylight Monday morning.

For our daytime stakeouts, we needed more stealth. There was already an observation deck available for the flood plain environmental area behind the dam, but that seemed too

235

obvious, and cops or FBI agents sitting up there in the daytime (or even worse, at night) would be a big stop sign for our perp. So we opted for camouflaged deer hunting stands. Those were common throughout Texas, and we arranged through the Texas Parks and Wildlife Department to borrow several. The deer blinds were unobtrusive, and we were hoping that Smithson would think they were just part of the observation tools being used by the environmentalists. By ten AM Monday morning we had everything in place. The deer blinds were small, and we didn't want too much traffic in the area, so we just staffed each stand with one person, on rotating shifts. That way there was never more than one person walking in or walking out of the marsh at any one time.

Two people per blind would have been better, so that they could backup each other, but there just wasn't room in the blinds, so we had to make do. Too big a crowd would scare Smithson off, too. We made sure everyone was well armed. If Smithson showed up, everyone had enough firepower to stop him - one way or another. We also issued everyone cameras and binoculars, so that if Smithson was watching the area, it would look like photographers checking out the birds and wildlife, and not a stakeout. We were as prepared as we could get - but we didn't know for sure that he was coming to the party. Doing all of this on a hunch was either going to be the smartest move I ever made, or end up being what one of my early bosses called a "career truncation move."

James Smith
Journal Entry
Monday November 27, 2006

I've got all my Semtex charges prepared, and I'm ready to place them. It takes "shaped" charges to penetrate deep into concrete, so I had to mold my plastic explosives into coffee cans, to force the explosive power into a single direction (out the opening of the can, the path of least resistance). I've decided on a two-pronged approach. To make sure the dam is breached, I need explosives on both sides of the dam, in the water on the lake side of the dam and on the downstream side, going off at the exact same time. All my charges will be set near the conduit that is already there. The idea is to force cracks in the concrete surrounding the conduit throughout the width of the dam. If that occurs, the water pressure will push through the cracks, widening them, and the dam will fail at that point. As soon as there is an opening, the water pressure will start widening the hole. Within minutes the entire spillway could go, and there will be tons of water flowing down the old river bed.

I had a tough time figuring out how to waterproof the charges I want to use on the lake side of the dam, but I finally realized that the solution was simple. Zip Lock bags are waterproof, and every grocery store sells them in sizes large enough to hold a pound or two of explosives. I had enough detonators and timers for 10 more charges, so I split those in the bags, too. I was going to have to set my timers far enough in advance to get in, set my charges, get back out, and hit the other side of the dam. Since my timers are of the 24 hour variety, everything has to be put in place during the same day and night. I've called the marina, and rented a boat for this afternoon. If I can get those charges in place, the backside of the dam should be much easier to get to, and the charges there will be much easier to place. I want the charges going off late at night as usual, to make sure my targets are at home, snug in their beds. Unless they are wearing lifejackets to bed, they will probably get to sleep forever after tonight. Is this what the Mafia means by "Sleeping with the fishes?"

I hate wasting all of my remaining explosives on a pipsqueak irritant like Peterson, but he is in the way of me completing my mission, and the flood strategy is straight out of Exodus. My goal is in sight. Completing my mission is still my major focus. To paraphrase Margaret Mitchell's favorite southern belle, "As God is my witness, if I can complete this task, I'll never be hungry again." Hungry for revenge, that is. I know I've sold my soul to the devil, and to get it back I have to succeed. Nothing else matters! If I can get rid of Peterson, I will then have more time to find a way to get some of the Bush family exposed to a few of my remaining toys.

And now it is even more personal between me and Billy P. This afternoon the news carried the story of my Mom's death. She died of a pill overdose, and the police are saying that the initial indications are that this was a planned suicide. I don't know if it depression over my Dad's death that finally pushed her over the edge, if it was an accident that just looks like a suicide, or if she was so ashamed of my failures to succeed in what I am trying to accomplish that she just felt she couldn't face it anymore. She always told me that she would be proud of me no matter what path I took, so I knew that she was already upstairs in Heaven, trying to figure out how she could help me finish what I have started down here on earth. She was a great Mom, and I miss her already. And the way things are, I can't even go to her funeral. I'll just have to visit her grave sometime in the future, and say my goodbyes then.

The more I think about how this is turning out, the madder I get! I know that I could have blown that luxury box if Peterson had not interrupted me, and by now George Bush might be so deep in grief that he might be considering suicide. So I have even more reasons to try and get rid of Peterson. I wrote, "This one's for Mom" on the bottom of one of the bombs I'm placing by the dam. I hope Peterson gets the message.

I know the rest of Peterson's team will still keep coming after me, even if I succeed in washing his body down to the Gulf, but they don't seem to be as sharp as he is. On the political side of this, things are actually looking up a little. Bush surprisingly mentioned me in his Saturday speech, asking that I give myself up before more people are injured. He said that he is working to get our troops out of Iraq just as fast as possible. I still don't think he understands how to think out of the box, and that he is considering every possible alternative solution. I want our people home now, not in a year or two. Let the Shiites and Sunnis and Kurds fight their sectarian civil war in the Middle East. It would serve them right if they used up so many of their own people and resources that they ended up getting absorbed by Iran. We tried to form a democracy over there, and that experiment has failed. So give up and get out!

I'm glad Bush is at least thinking about me and my agenda. I want to keep it fresh on his mind, and blowing this dam just a few miles from his ranch will show him just how powerless he is to stop me from succeeding. It is God's will that I succeed, so I know that ultimately nothing can stop me. I will prevail, and our troops will get pulled from that horrible mistake of a war. If you don't believe me, just go ask the Vice-President. I wonder if they have finally found all of him under all of that snow? I wonder if they will be able to find Peterson after I give him the bath I have planned for him?

I guess I will have to write another letter to the remaining members of his team, explaining why I hit Waco. I'm not sure they will be able to figure it out without some assistance. I'll have to come up with some sort of nautical reference because of the flood, or maybe quote something from Noah's adventure as told in Genesis. That might be more logical than "damn the torpedoes," or "I have just begun to fight." Maybe just a casual reference to the Nile waters closing over the Egyptian army, as the Hebrews escaped into the wilderness. I'll have time to figure my message wording out after I get the charges in place. I want to get this done before Peterson decides to move to Crawford, or goes back to Washington. The story in the paper said he would be in Waco with his wife for a few more days. Maybe I ought to just call him, and sing him a lullaby to help him sleep. "Row, row, row your boat, gently down the stream" seems appropriate.

Bill Peterson
Waco Regional Airport
11:45 AM Monday, November 27, 2006

I have set up our control point in the airport tower, so that we have a great view of the spillway area on the lake and the airport perimeter road near the dam. We have our people in place, just waiting for our guy to show his face. Unfortunately, there are a lot more people in the area than I would like. There are a

241

lot of boats on the water. One of the air traffic controllers here in the tower is an avid fisherman, and he told me the striper fishing was great this time of year in the deep water next to the dam - so there are boats trolling back and forth across our entire target area. One of those boats is ours, and our people are surreptitiously checking out the "fishermen" on the other boats. I'm not happy with the situation, but we can't shut down the lake without scaring Smithson away. Under these conditions, it is possible that Smithson could lay his charges right under our noses in that deep water next to the spillway.

There are more people than I would like on the environmental site on the back side of the dam, too. Apparently the week between Thanksgiving and finals is a great time to come check out your field site - so a lot of would-be environmental undergrad and potential PhD types are out there, oohing and aahing over the birds, the small mammals, and even the weeds. They would freak if they knew what kind of big game we were hunting in their playground. I was hoping to use infrared and heat-seeking scopes and cameras in the area, to help us capture this turkey. But with so many people in the area, I don't think the extra scopes would help. We would just end up catching some biologist wandering blissfully from nest to nest.

I got a phone call from my new boss early this morning, asking me why my ego had gotten so big that I thought I might be a target. Actually, his language was a little more colorful than that, with a few adjectives describing the level of my IQ thrown in for good measure. It was pretty obvious that he was not a happy camper. I told him that I really have no justification for the way I feel - I'm going just on gut instinct, and the flood story from Exodus. He told me he would give our little effort 48 hours, and then he was going to shut it down as too costly, and put our people back helping to guard the Bush family.

He ended by saying, "They are the real targets. When you get yourself elected to office, then maybe you can make enemies like this guy Smithson. Until then, don't let your success in Austin go to your head. After all, you had the guy right in front of you, and you let him get away. If this guy doesn't show today or tomorrow, I'm going to pull the plug on your little flaky flood party down there."

Obviously the honeymoon period between us was over, and I had better produce.

I keep having thoughts on how Smithson might do this. Looking at an area map, I saw that there is an area on the lake past the Marina leased to the Waco model airplane club. That reminded me of what he had tried in Austin. Would he try the airplane trick again? I didn't think he could get enough explosives into the plane to even dent the dam, but he could fly it through a window at Margaret's house? And how about a real plane, and possibly using that aircraft as a flying bomb? That trick has been tried before

243

in New York, with some success. I can't see him as a suicide hijacker, but anything is possible. Would even a plane full of explosives put a dent in this dam? Have I covered every possibility? Is there some other way he can get to the dam that I haven't considered, or planned for? Is he even coming at all, or is this just another wild goose chase, and my team is just like the environmentalists, chasing our tail feathers?

James Smith
Journal Entry
Monday, November 27, 2006

The charges on the lake side of the dam are in place. I couldn't use shaped charges on that side, because the bags were rotating in the water as I let out my fishing line, and there was no way to tell which way the charges were facing when I got them on the bottom. I put weights in the bottom of the coffee cans, to help get the explosives to the bottom more quickly, and to hold them in place when I unhooked the cans from my fishing line. I think I have enough firepower at the spillway entrance to take the dam down, even if the cans are not facing in the right direction, if I can get the charges on the back side of the dam go off at the same time. It was difficult getting those charges down to the right location. I had to really try and catch fish with one line, while dropping charges with the other fishing line on the dam of the boat. Most boats had two or more people in them - one driving, while the other watched the trolling lines. But there were a few "singles" like me out there, trying to do it alone. It was cold enough on the water that I could keep a lot of clothes up around my face. Hopefully that was enough to keep anyone from recognizing me from another boat, and I tried to keep my distance as much as possible from the other fishermen. It took most of the day, and a lot of passes along the dam, to get all of my charges where I wanted them. "Trolling" with a bag containing plastic explosives and dynamite is not my normal fishing trip.

In some places in the south, the rednecks still fish with dynamite - you explode a stick of dynamite deep in the water, and the stunned fish will float to the surface. If you think the game warden would disapprove of fishing with explosives, just imagine what he would think if he searched my boat, and found enough explosives to bring up half the fish in this huge lake? I tried to maintain a low profile, just in case some Texas Game Warden might be inclined to stop me to check my catch.

There is an old joke about the guy that went fishing with his local game warden. The redneck lit a stick of dynamite, tossed it in the water, and bang! Fish started floating.

The game warden said, "You can't do that! Fishing with dynamite is illegal around here!"

The redneck lit another stick of dynamite, and handed it to the game warden. "Are you going to just sit there and complain, or are you going to fish?"

After finishing laying the charges in the water, I took the boat back to the marina, and headed for the marshy area off of North 19th Street. But it looked like a convention at the parking lot there! People were coming and going, with cameras, dip nets, collection bottles, and other outdoor experimental site paraphernalia. I remember seeing on the lake Website the info about the outdoor science lab site, but I didn't expect this many people there the week after Thanksgiving. If anything, I had expected the site to be deserted!

I had taken environmental science back in high school, so I had a general idea what they were doing - and they were going to be in my way if I tried to place my explosives during daylight. So I came back to my motel, to rest up and wait until it gets dark. I'm passing the time catching up on my sleep, checking the Internet for news about me or Peterson, and putting my thoughts in this journal. After tonight, I may mail this to Peterson's office. Perhaps some of his FBI counterparts will get a kick knowing how I felt about him, and how Peterson didn't have a clue that I had decided to target him before I went back after the President.

I had actually thought about sending him a warning letter. But he is way too sharp, and would have guessed why he was now getting a copy of the letter. And if I said anything about water, he would deduce my plan before I could put any of it in place. So I will keep quiet, and maybe send this after I blow the joint. I did drive by his mother-in-law's place this afternoon, and Peterson's car was sitting in the driveway. So it looks like my target is still in town, unaware of my plans, and available for my oversized car wash.

Bill Peterson
Waco Lake Research Area parking lot
9:58 PM Monday, November 27, 2006

I was standing in the shadows at the edge of the parking lot, waiting on my relief (and my ride) to show up, when a car pulled into the lot and slowed. It wasn't the car I was expecting. But right behind it, my car did pull in. And as soon as the first car saw the headlights from the second one behind it, the first car headed back out. It was either teenagers coming to the lot to drink, smoke pot, or make out (or all of the above - not everyone in Waco is a staunch Baptist), or else it was Smithson coming to set his charges. It was just bad timing that he showed just when our car pool vehicle showed, or else we might have captured him right then. If it was him. Maybe I'm reading way too much into everything. It was probably just kids, out for a little fun, and we ruined that, too.

It was too dark to get the year of the car - it looked like an early '90's Chrysler model. I couldn't see the license plates from where I was standing in the bushes. We didn't have enough information to track that car down, no matter who was driving. But it did give me hope that our trap might work. After seeing the wood duck lovers all day, I had come to the conclusion that if Smithson was coming, he would be coming after dark. Seeing that car had reinforced my assumption, and I radioed my team to stay alert. I decided that I would come back for the 2 AM shift myself. A good leader doesn't ask his team to do anything he is not willing to do himself, and the team leader shouldn't wallow in the perks that come with being the boss. You have to get down and dirty with the troops sometimes. In this case, that meant getting cold in a deer blind in the middle of the night.

The people in the blinds were now better prepared for catching our guy, and we had a lot of support available. Mark Simpson had told the President what we were trying to do, and the President had told Robert Gates, the new appointee as Secretary of Defense. Gates had been in the stadium on Friday, and was now apparently one of our team's admirers. He had Fort Hood dispatch 30 sets of state-of-the-art night vision goggles, rifles with infrared and laser sights, and higher quality pocket heaters for all of our stakeout people to use. There was even a team of Green Berets rotating through the airport tower with 24 hour coverage, ready to help track this guy in case we spotted him, and to help make sure he wouldn't get away again. I'm halfway surprised we didn't have an entire battalion with tanks doing night exercises around the dam. I've issued orders to consider Smithson armed and dangerous. I don't want anyone trying to be nice to this guy, thinking that he is just another maladjusted kid that could be saved with some long-term psychological help. I remember the old "Boys Town" movie, where the priest said, "There's no such thing as a bad boy." Apparently he hasn't met some of the people I've run into over the years. Smithson knows what he is doing, so when he is caught, he will need to pay his debt to society. If we don't kill him trying to capture him, I hope that means some jury will give him the death penalty. I would be happy to do the injections, or throw the switch on the electric chair, if someone would allow me that opportunity.

James Smith
Journal Entry
Monday, November 27, 2006

The car coming into the parking lot behind me, right after I pulled into the lot, scared me. I expected to be alone at that time of night, but when the other car showed up I panicked and bolted. I don't know if it was some Good Samaritan checking on me, kids looking for a place to be alone, or some sort of law enforcement operation checking on the dam. I don't see how they could know I am here. Maybe I'm getting too paranoid. But just to make sure,

I'm changing my modus operandi. I'm going to sneak in along the airport perimeter road, instead of taking the logical way through the marsh. Since the airport is already allegedly "secure," with no one being allowed on the tarmac without permission, I don't think anyone watching from there will be as alert as someone in the marsh might be. The marsh may not be a problem. It could be that it was just some late night pond observer coming to check a nest. But I can't take that chance, so I am going to do it the hard way. My dad trained me to make it to your goal, no matter what has to be done - so I know I can get there, even if I have to crawl all the way in to my target area.

Speaking of my dad, and my mission to memorialize his death by forcing our politicians to bring our troops home, I heard on the radio today that a plan is being developed to turn over more of Iraq to the Iraqi security forces, which will allow us to move out of some of the more volatile areas of that country. My mission may finally be succeeding! But Peterson still needs to go. He has gotten in my way too many times, and his 9 lives are up. At 4 AM, the dam will go, and by 4:10 Jerusalem on the Brazos may be a few miles further downstream than it was. I still have to get these last few charges planted, and I can fade into the woodwork in Brisbane or the Cook Islands. Who knows - in a few years I may start my own lab. I've proven I can handle viruses well, and make them do as I please. I'm sure there will be a market for that skill somewhere in the world. Instead of Moses, maybe I need to be known as Doctor Strangelove. But I can't see Peterson as a James Bond type. After tonight, Waco may need a new hero.

Bill Peterson
Waco Lake Research Area parking lot
2:10 AM Tuesday, November 28, 2006

I'm worried, and trying not to panic. Sally was supposed to meet me in the parking lot at 2 AM sharp. I was going to the blind, and she was going back to her motel room to bed, her shift completed. She hasn't shown, and she is not answering my calls on our communications system. I got on the mike. "Heads up, everybody. We may have a situation here. Sally hasn't made the changing of the guard. I want two of the guys from the airport to start moving toward the marsh. Be careful who you shoot, because I'm going in from this direction." I got two clicks on the mike, meaning order understood and being carried out. I pulled my weapon, the FBI standard Colt 10mm I have been carrying for the last few years. I wasn't using a flashlight, because I didn't want to scare off our potential target. However, the light in the parking lot had ruined my night vision, and it took me a few minutes before I could see well enough to start edging along the trail into the brush.

251

I'm pretty stealthy when I want to be. I grew up hunting small game and deer here in Texas, and even though we mostly hunt deer from tree stands, I do know how to stalk. We Texas hunters know how to trail turkeys, hogs, and almost anything else that can be found in the wild that can be eaten. I can be quiet, and I know how to watch my step so that I'm not walking on crackling sticks or rustling leaves and making myself obvious to everyone, and everything, already in the woods. As long as I could hear the noises of the night birds and insects around me, meager as they were this time of year, I knew I was being quiet enough. So when the noises stopped, I knew that either I had made a blunder, or someone else had alarmed the local residents enough to make them shut up. I had gotten to within about 50 feet of our first deer blind, and still could not see Sally. Then my communicator went off in my ear.

All I heard was a voice I didn't know saying, "Turn your cell phone back on."

I stood still for what seemed like 10 minutes, but was probably only a few seconds. I didn't want my cell phone ringer going off, telling anyone in the woods where I was standing, but I knew somehow that this was Smithson, and he probably knew that I was approaching the blind. I knew that he had Sally's communicator, and he wanted to talk, but he didn't want what he had to say to be overheard by everyone on our communication circuit. I eased my cell phone out of my pocket, turned it on, and immediately switched it to vibrator mode. When it started buzzing, I answered it quietly.

"Hello? Who is this?"

"Well hello, Mr. big shot FBI man. Don't think you are going to get out of this one as easily as you did down in Austin. I think you know who I am. What is important is that I have your female agent, and she's going with me all the way out. If you want her to live, back away from the blind." I told him to give me a few minutes, and that I would call him back when I had moved back toward the parking lot. He said, "Don't take too long or we will all be swimming." I hung up the phone.

We were in trouble, and I knew it. We had a hostage situation out here in the woods, in the dark, downstream from a dam that might be wired to blow in a few minutes, and the bad guy had a copy of our communicator. I did have my cell phone, and he couldn't listen in on that, so I turned off my Secret Service communicator and started calling for help using the cell. I got Andy Livingston on the phone, and explained the situation to him as tersely as possible. I told him we needed a new communication system on a different frequency, we needed people to start searching for bombs, in case Smithson had already planted them, and we needed a SWAT team and the Green Berets to help save Sally. I knew help would arrive fairly quickly. The question was would it be quick enough to save Sally, and possibly to save Waco.

I really had not retreated very far from where I got the first call. I called Smithson back on my cell, and told him, "You say you have my agent. Prove it. Let me talk to her."

I heard what sounded like tape being ripped, and then I heard her voice. She said softly, "Bill?"

"Sally? Are you OK?"

That one word from her was all I got before Smithson was back on his phone. "OK, now do you believe me? And don't start pulling all of that hostage negotiator stalling for time bullshit. We've got less than two hours before that dam blows, and I don't plan on being here when that happens. Do you understand me, Agent Peterson?"

"I understand. What do you want?"

"Safe passage out of here, obviously. And she goes with me until I'm sure I'm away from all of your tricks. I have nothing against her. It's you I'm upset with."

The Academy course on hostage negotiation teaches us that in situations like this, to keep the guy talking. If he is talking, he is not thinking, and not panicking. A panicked guy with a gun is the worst case hostage scenario. As long as he is talking, there is a chance of ending the situation peaceably. I tried to follow that scenario, but I think he had read the same textbook.

I said, "I'm sorry you're upset with me, and I'm sorry about the death of your father. Tell me about him. I know his death is the reason you have been doing this. I read that he was quite a hero in the army."

He laughed, but it sounded like that last sip of coffee from an urn that has been left on the burner too long. He said, "We don't have time for that. In about 90 minutes that dam is going to go, and I don't want to be still standing here, downstream from the spillway." That got my attention. Unless he was bluffing, he had already set his charges on this side of the dam. I asked, "Don't you still need to do the lakeside?"

He said, "Did that yesterday. My dad taught me how to fish, along with everything else that was worth learning."

Just trying to keep the conversation going, I asked, "Why did you decide to come after me and my family?"

Smithson laughed again. "You were getting too good at guessing what I would do next. You know me too well, so you had to go. You being here tonight is proof of that. Nothing personal, although I didn't like you turning the letter I sent you over to the press."

I told him, "You do realize that with the power in Congress changing to the Democrats, and Rumsfeld gone, you are getting what you wanted - before long we will be bringing troops home?"

"No guarantees of that," he sighed, "If I could be sure of that, I would have stopped the plagues and traded in this life for one much more pastoral."

Then it hit me. Trading was the key. "Robert - is it OK if I call you Robert? How about we try this? I come in there, unarmed, and you trade her for me. If I come in there, will you let her go? If it is me you want, here's your chance. What do you say? Can we make a deal?"

It was quiet for a long moment. Then he said, "Why not? I have to trust you to come in here peaceably, which I don't, and you have to trust me to let her go after you get in here, and I'm sure you don't trust me, either. But at least if you are in here, you are not out there scheming against me. I don't have a thing against her, so if I have to kill a hostage, I would rather it be you. OK, if you come in, I'll let her go - and you don't have any reasons to distrust me. I've always done exactly what I said I was going to do. And you know I had my reasons for doing what I did. I do need to make sure you are not armed. What I want you to do is strip, and walk to the door of the blind buck naked with your hands in the air. I promise I won't shoot you if you don't come in armed, and try and pull anything on the way in."

I heard two clicks on my communicator earpiece. I knew that Smithson had been raised as an army brat, and would know that the clicks meant the Green Berets were now in position, but I didn't know if Smithson had been listening to both the communicator and the cell phone at the same time. I was hoping he had missed the clicks, and wouldn't realize that anyone else was already on site. Listening to the communicator would have been difficult while he was talking, so I decided that his offer was a chance worth taking.

"OK," I told him on the phone, "I'm stripping." I tried to do that as quickly as possible, but it wasn't easy taking clothes off in the cold, with nothing around but a few straggly Mesquite trees.

I did leave my boots on. Walking through that brush in the cold was going to be bad enough, and I didn't want to try it barefooted in the dark. I knew that Smithson could see me, because he had Sally's night-vision goggles. How he had captured her when she had the night vision advantage was beyond me, but maybe he really was trained better than I thought. Maybe he had bought his own pair at some army surplus location that sold gear like that. I was sure that he had no problem seeing me. All of these thoughts were going through my head as I dropped my pants, took a deep breath, and turned back toward the deer blind.

Then I stopped. I had been waiting for a light to go off, for a plan to come to me. What I really needed was a bright light to go off, right in Smithson's eyes, and I had one with me. I bent over, and picked up my still turned off flashlight. It was a big MagLight, weighing about 3 or 4 pounds with the 4 "D" batteries it held. The ads for that light said it could be seen for half a mile. I only needed it to work for a distance of about six inches. I took my own night vision goggles off, turned on the flashlight, but kept the lens covered with my hand. The light escaping from the lens was bright enough for me to see where I was going, but that was about it. I kept it pointed toward the ground, even turning it a little to my rear, to cut the lumens that Smithson could see. I headed down the trail for the blind.

I didn't want the guy to be able to think about it too much, so as I approached the deer blind I turned the flashlight back off, and called him back one more time with the cell phone. I wanted to let him know I was coming in, and to please not shoot me until we had a chance to talk. I moved as quickly as possible without seeming to be hurrying, trying to keep him on the phone at the same time. It only took me about 15 seconds to reach the door to the blind. There was a small window-type opening on the door side, as there was on every side of the deer blind, to allow hunters to see in every direction. I knew Smithson would be watching me through that opening.

My guess, and my hope, was that he had Sally tied up somehow, either using tape or rope, and that he would be pointing his weapon at me instead of her, thinking that I was the greater danger at that moment. I hoped I was the greater danger, too. As I reached the door, I swung my flashlight up, turning it back on, and put the beam flush in the window opening by the door, and hopefully right in Smithson's eyes. At the same time I kicked in the door with my right boot, hoping to upset his aim. The idea was to blind him with the light, if he was wearing the night vision goggles. I heard a scream, but I couldn't be sure if the scream came from him or me. And then the gun went off as I dove through the door.

I saw him frantically trying to get the goggles off his head. I jumped on top of him, hitting him right between the eyes with the barrel of the flashlight, and grabbed for his gun. The hood for the night vision goggles kept me from braining him with the flashlight. He wasn't anywhere as big as I was, but he knew how to fight. The first thing he did was try to kick me in the balls. I managed to turn a little, so that he missed the vital spot. I was focusing on getting control of the gun, still in his right hand, and hoping that he wouldn't keep firing the thing at random. I had my left hand on the gun, hitting him with the flashlight with my right, and trying to keep him from getting at me at the same time. It was a fun few seconds. At 6-4, I had a good bit of leverage on him, and it didn't take me long to wrestle the gun from him. But even before I could point it at him, he knocked me back to the ground with a leg sweep, and jumped for the doorway.

I started to shoot him, but I just couldn't bring myself to shoot an unarmed guy. As it turned out, I didn't have to. The door opening was filled with one of the biggest guys I had ever

259

seen, one of the Green Beret Sergeants. He zapped Smithson with a Taser, and Smithson went down, folding up the way a kite falls when the wind dies. He collapsed to the ground, and we finally had our guy.

The Sergeant was taking care of Smithson, checking to make sure he was really out, and looking for additional weapons, so I looked around for Sally. She was crumpled in the far corner of the blind, her hands and legs tied with duct tape. There was also tape over her mouth and eyes. I was worried sick that she had been shot when I crashed through the door. I lifted her head up, looking for wounds, but I didn't see any. She stirred as I tried to gently take the tape off of her mouth, and then her eyes.

She blinked in the light from the flashlights, looked at me, and then grinned. "This approach won't get you in my pants, either. I've never been into getting tied up and getting kinky." That is when I realized that I was standing there in nothing but my boots. Before I could even ask her if she was OK she looked me up and down again. "And just exactly how cold is it outside?" was her next crack. I didn't even bother to untie her hands. I turned, picked up my cell phone and flashlight, and walked out of the blind, headed for my clothes. I may not have exactly been a knight in shining armor, but she didn't have to insult me after I rescued her. And if she was hurling insults, then she wasn't hurt. Thank God for small favors!

I could hear sirens in the distance. One part of the dance was over, but we still had the major problem of the wired dam, ready to blow, and our source of information on where the bombs were placed now had his brains scrambled from the Taser. He would regain consciousness eventually, but I didn't know if we could get any information out of him when he did. Andy Livingston had notified the Green Berets, and then called the rest of the team, the local police, EMTs (they were taking care of Sally), the Waco SWAT team, the police EOD team, and even Fort Hood. The problem was that it was now three AM, and we only had an hour or so until the dam was scheduled to be taken out, if Smithson was sticking to his usual four AM game time. We had to find the bombs, get them defused, and clear the area before four. I told everybody to grab their low light gear and their flashlights, and we all headed for the spillway.

We didn't know how many bombs Smithson had set, but they had to be either close to the conduit, or along the Spillway itself. I didn't think there was anything we could do about the bombs, if there really were any, on the lake side of the dam. But Bill Erickson thought that if he and a couple of other guys tried trolling slowly along the dam with heavy lines and big treble hooks, they might could hook onto a couple of the

261

bombs, and at least get them away from the base of the dam. I told him to give it a try, but to be careful - I didn't want him blowing himself up, and starting the explosion sequence early. I also told him to make sure they cleared the area no later than 0345. He took Charlie and Andy with him, and they headed for the marina to grab a boat and gear.

By this time we had about 20 people on the scene, on the backside of the spillway. Since it is about 500 feet long, that gave us about 25 feet each to inspect - too much area to do a decent job, especially in the dark, and even more difficult if Smithson had buried his bombs, or actually put them in the shallow water in the conduit. Someone from the local force handed me a cell phone, and asked that I talk to their Chief of Police. I told him the situation, and he said he would start immediate evacuations downstream, starting with the area closest to the dam. I told him he had better hurry. I took the people we had on hand, divided them up, and we started walking the spillway area. Marty found one bomb almost immediately. It was in a coffee can, in a shallow hole right next to where the conduit came through the spillway wall, on the northwest side of the conduit. We knew there had to be more than that one.

But the rest of the bombs, if there were more bombs, couldn't be found. The police were bringing in bomb-sniffing dogs, but I wasn't sure they would get to us in time to do any good, or if they would be able to smell the explosives if they were in the water. We went up and down, back and forth - but no luck. We couldn't find any disturbed earth, where someone might have been digging. No bombs buried under a pile of rocks, which is sometimes used to help shape the force and direction of the blast. Nothing! It was now approaching 3:30 AM, close to the time I wanted our people evacuated. The only place we had not searched was in the water itself - the shallow stream coming through the conduit. If there were one or more bombs in that tunnel, and if they went off with us nearby, the blast wave coming out of the tunnel would probably blow us half way to Houston. We had to look in the water, but we had to do it quickly.

We tried wading, but no luck using our hands and feet to feel for bags of explosives or coffee cans. We couldn't see underwater at all - the flashlights just reflected off the top of the stream. It was damn cold and uncomfortable in the water, and I was about to give up and have everyone evacuate the area, when one of the Green Berets came up. The same sergeant that had zapped Smithson said, "Sir, I don't know if you are aware of it, but these new lowlight goggles are guaranteed waterproof for up to 30 minutes, and can gather light underwater just as well as above water. You might want to try searching in the water using these."

I had never considered trying the goggles underwater. I put a pair on, and stuck my head under the cold water. I could see about 8 feet, much better than we were doing on our own. I came back up, and told everybody that could get a set and was willing to volunteer to search in the water to get them on and get going. We soon had 6 people searching, and it wasn't long before we found our first bomb in the water. That was encouraging, but we were running out of time. At 3:45 I was going to clear everyone out. By 3:43 we had found two more bombs, and I told everyone in the water to start moving. The guys on the boat had lucked out, and snagged two bombs along the base of the dam on their side. We knew there were probably more, but we were out of time. All we could do is hope we had done enough.

We cleared back to the airport tower, on higher ground, and far enough from the dam that the bomb squad people thought we would be safe. The EOD team had disarmed all the bombs we had found. The arming mechanism that Smithson had set up was simple, and all that needed to be done was to pull the arming wires and the timer away from the explosives. Speaking of Smithson, he was coming around. He was in handcuffs and shackles, and being guarded by a mixed team of cops, army people, and FBI agents in a room on the bottom floor of the tower. I went in to see him.

"How many bombs did you set?"

"I dropped five on the water side, and 5 on the downstream side. The idea was to set up sympathetic blast waves through the concrete, cracking it all the way through."

Sally was back from her visit with the medics. She had a bump on her head, but she had refused to go to the hospital. She asked, "Was everything set to go at four AM?"

"Yep. I wanted to catch as many people home as possible, including Agent Peterson, here."

The Waco Police Chief, a guy named Roland, came in and said, "We've had a good bit of success evacuating people, using a combination of fire, rescue, and police going door to door. But if the entire dam goes, there are still going to be a lot of fatalities."

We all looked at each other, and almost simultaneously looked at our watches. 3:58 AM.

Waco, Texas
4:00 AM Tuesday, November 28, 2006

I could almost hear the timers on the remaining bombs counted down to zero. I could see in my mind the relays opening paths, electrons flowing, and ignition starting. I could feel energy starting to expand from the heart of each bag. I imagined the pressure waves starting to build, and in milliseconds the bags were no more, and the blast waves were being directed against the walls of the dam. The reality was a pretty strong blast, but actually not quite as bad as my imagination. We could feel the building we

265

were in sway even as far away as we were from the explosions. We had the Army overhead in helicopters by this time, and they were observing from a safe enough height and distance the blast wave would not reach them.

The first report came in on the airport radio from one of the Fort Hood helicopter crews. "Looks like 3 blasts on the water side, and one on the downstream side. No sign yet of a major breach in the spillway wall." We all knew that sometimes breaches can take a while before the water pressure can force its way through. The immediate situation was not great, but better than it could have been. I had been holding my breath, and I let it all out in one long whoosh. We weren't completely out of the woods, but at least the entire lake wasn't already racing downstream, straight through town, heading for the Gulf of Mexico.

As soon as the smoke cleared a little, we got low light video of the back side of the dam. There were a few cracks in the conduit, but I didn't see any increased water flow. But then a piece of concrete fell from the base of the spillway into the conduit, almost in slow motion. There were a lot of bubbles in the water, and the stream coming out from under the dam suddenly grew a little wider.

"Oh, shit," said Chief Roland. I wondered if the Chief of Police in Waco was allowed to cuss, but I didn't say anything. The stream doubled its volume again, and a little more concrete fell. The ponds and the observation tower downstream of the dam disappeared as the creek grew in size to where it resembled a small river more than a creek.

But then the old/new river quit growing. It was now about a 25 foot wide stream coming out from beneath the spillway, with a lot of rapids in the water, but it wasn't getting any noticeably wider. I felt like I could breathe again. Lt. Lloyd Adams, the guy from the Corps of Engineers that had showed us the dam Sunday night, had joined us. He added his expertise. He told us that there was still a chance of further concrete deterioration as the pressure built in the conduit, but unless the cracking was severe, we were probably seeing maximum water flow. He also said that the damage could be repaired, but that it would take months.

Bill Erickson said, "It looks right now like fun white water out there, directly downstream from the dam. You could leave it as it is, and make it a kayaking and canoeing recreational area."

Adams said that would be fine with him, but that decision would obviously have to come from much higher up the chain of command in the Corps of Engineers.

The Lieutenant asked Chief Roland how much damage would be done downstream by the increased water flow.

Roland said, "Not much. We have easements on the stream bed wide enough to handle most of the extra water. We have city rules that say no human habitation can be built in the streambed. There will be a few storage sheds, some fences, and small barns that may be damaged, and maybe some livestock lost, but overall this is not a serious catastrophe."

Chief Roland reached over and shook my hand. "Thanks for helping to save our town."

"Well, Chief, I'm sorry this asshole decided to follow me here, but at least we finally have him in custody. I appreciate your folks helping us with him."

"No problem," said the Chief. "Glad to help. Do you want us to hold him for you here, or are you taking him directly into Federal custody?"

I hadn't even considered what to do with Smithson now that we had him, and the immediate crisis was over. I decided we had better hang on to him while we had him - I didn't want any custody fights over who got to try him first. "We'll keep him, Chief. I'll have the army guys assist our agents, and we'll take him to Ft. Hood. I imagine FBI headquarters will want him flown to D.C. as soon as possible, and that will be easier to handle from the military base. I'll make sure your assistance is noted in our report. Thanks again for your help."

And with that I wandered out of the tower building. It was cold, and I was still a little wet from looking for bombs in the water. But I had a phone call to make, and I didn't want to be overheard. I called Julie at her Aunt's place in

Dallas. Her Aunt Martha didn't like having to wake Julie up to talk to me, but Julie had heard the phone ring, and picked up the extension.

I said, "Hi sweetheart. I know it is 5 in the morning, but I wanted you to know we got him. Yes, we really have him this time. He managed to blow a small hole in the dam, but everything is going to be fine. There will not be any major downstream damage. I just wanted you to know that it's over, and that I love you more than you will ever know. You can come back to Waco anytime now." I heard her crying as she hung up the phone to go tell her Mom.

We would still have a trial to go through, unless some judge decided that Smithson was too crazy to stand trial. Tonight was an ending to a terrible phase in our life. I knew we would never forget, but it was time to move forward. And I knew what I wanted to do now that this part of my life was over.

Epilogue

Bill Peterson
FBI Headquarters
4:28 PM Wednesday, January 3, 2007

I was finishing a cup of coffee, admiring how clean my desk top looked for a change, when Sally Caruthers and Bill Erickson came walking into my office.

She said, "About done?"

"I've got one more box of stuff to take down to the car, and I'm out of here," I replied.

Erickson said, "Well, the Secret Service's gain will be the FBI's loss."

I said, "I hope so. I know there will be stress in that job, too - but at least I will be working where I'm wanted. Mark Sullivan said the President asked about me coming over there himself. And Mark and I have always gotten along fine. I'll still be in law enforcement, and will be working on counter-terrorism with their people, too, and that's always been my main interest."

Sally asked me, "Is Julie happy with the change?"

"She thinks it's a great opportunity. She's quitting the State Department. Now that she's pregnant again, she's ready to start decorating a nursery. And then she wants to be a full-time mom for a while. When she does want to go back to work, if she decides to go back, she won't have a problem finding a job. She has a graduate degree from the LBJ School of Public Affairs, and that will get her hired anywhere in this town."

Erickson and Sally looked at each other, and then back at me.

Sally said, "We wanted you to be one of the first to know," as she showed me the diamond on her left hand. "Bill gave it to me New Year's Eve at midnight. We're planning a June wedding, and we want both you and Julie to be there."

I grinned. "Wow. Congratulations. But this is a little sudden, don't you think?"

Sally smiled. "Well, we have been through a lot together. And everyone is saying that Bill is a shoe-in for the Pulitzer for his series on Smithson. You giving Bill first shot at the Smithson journal when we found it will make his career. We can never thank you enough for that. Not to mention you saving my life back in Waco."

I smiled, too, and then tried to look serious. "Just doing my job, ma'am. That's what we in the FBI are paid to do."

We all laughed.

I said to Erickson, "Bill, the one thing that bothers me a little is that your articles helped explain how crazy Smithson is, and that looks like it is going to help keep him locked up with Hinckley and Mark Chapman. Of course, half the world still thinks that the FBI and CIA were behind the assassination of John Lennon, so I don't know if using Chapman as a comparison is a fair one. Anyway, I would have liked to see Smithson fry. I felt he did know what he was doing, but did those things anyway, and so he deserves an Old Testament punishment since he is such a big Old Testament fan. Putting him in some psychiatric hospital, even a prison with a psychiatric wing, is not true justice for me, considering what this guy did to my family. Julie doesn't want him to die, and maybe she's a better Christian than I am. I don't want him enjoying life in any way. I think a lot of the families of the people he killed would like to see him get the death penalty, too. I can just see some psychiatrist in 20 years saying that Smithson is cured, and that he should be allowed back into society. Cindy Lester will never get that chance. Dick Cheney was denied the chance at a long life. Our baby never had a chance. Why should we even offer that possibility to Smithson? He is smart, and knows how to play the insanity game. He knows what he did was wrong. He is scum, and doesn't deserve to live. But the judge is already making noises about how a psychiatric defense motion might be favorably considered. What kind of crap is that?"

Sally said, "Bill, we did our jobs, and caught the guy. You know we can't control what the judicial system does with them after we get handcuffs on them."

I told her, "I know, but I can still wish he could suffer like he made so many people suffer. I know I can never forgive him. Yeah, I understand what you are saying about how we have to let cases go once they are out of our hands. But this one was too personal. Maybe I should have been pulled off the case after the Ricin incident."

Sally said, "You need to realize that you did at least have the satisfaction of helping to catch him. If Lawrence had pulled you off the case, all you would have is your frustration. Helping to bring him in should count for something, and I think in time you will realize that. You were part of a successful manhunt that might not have ended in a capture without your help. And think about all the people you helped to save along the way - that should count for something, too. And I know that you could have shot him in the deer blind, but you held back - and that shows that you do believe in letting people have their day in court." She patted my shoulder. "Bill, you will always be the best team leader I ever worked for, and I will remember this manhunt for the rest of my life."

It was time to change the subject. I told Erickson, "Bill, after what you did to help the team, you have more than met the challenge I gave you. You deserve whatever success you achieve from your write ups on what we accomplished."

He smiled, and just nodded his thanks. Sally looked at him, and tapped her watch. It would be interesting to see who was going to wear the pants in that family!

"Well, we have to be going, Erickson said. "I still want another interview with you once you're settled in the Service."

I shrugged, and took another sip of coffee. "I don't know, Bill. They don't call it 'Secret' for nothing."

He grinned and turned to go. I knew how persistent he could be. I was going to have to run his request by the public relations people at Secret Service headquarters. That should be interesting - their new hire asking about being interviewed? I didn't want my notoriety following me across town if at all possible. Both Julie and I wanted just to put this behind us, and move on with our lives. I'm sure that will be easier said than done, but I don't need a reporter keeping the story fresh in front of everyone else's eyes every day in the paper.

Sally walked around the desk and gave me a hug. As she was walking out behind her new fiancé, she turned, and in her best fake Australian accent, said, "No Wally's, mate."

I again nearly spit up the sip of coffee I had just taken. I started coughing and laughing at the same time.

Erickson stopped and said, "Shouldn't that be 'No worries?'"

Sally shook her head no, looked back at me, winked, and said, "Not in this case!"

ACKNOWLEDGEMENTS

I would like to thank several people for their assistance in getting this book published. Thanks to Jarrod Johnson for help with the science, Joanna Davis for her editing, and Julie for her encouragement.

The quote by Robert B. Kaplan is used with permission.

While there are several "real" people used as characters in this book, all of their actions, and the events and timelines used in the book are fictional. Some buildings and places have been moved to fit the story. Any errors are mine.

Thanks for reading, and if you enjoyed the book, please leave me a review on Amazon. If you are interested in obtaining television or movie rights for this or any of my other books, please contact me at jerryjohnson66@comcast.net.

My next book, SIX, a sequel to this book, will be out in the spring of 2018.

- Jerry Johnson